Swagger:

A Celebration of the Butch Experience

Curated by Rae Theodore

Edited by Nat Burns

Paperback ISBN: 978-1-61929-553-7
Hardback ISBN: 978-1-61929-552-0

Flashpoint Publications First Edition: June, 2024

Printed in the United States of America.

Cover design by TreeHouse Studio

www.flashpointpublications.com

Foreward

Butch. The word always felt solid to me. Something to hold onto when I wasn't sure about who I was. I knew there were others who had come before me and that this was the name they wore. When I first tried it on, butch felt like a well-worn flannel shirt or leather jacket. Butch felt like home.

I've been looking for books about butches ever since I came out nearly two decades ago. While I've read most that I've come across, I've always been surprised that there wasn't one book showcasing a variety of butch voices. It was that lack that sparked the idea for this one. I sent an e-mail to Patty Schramm, publisher of Flashpoint Publications, and we were off to the races. Once the submissions started coming in, I knew we had something special on our hands.

Our fearless writers shared their stories and their hearts and weighed in on what butch means to them. Through stories, poems, and essays, they tell what it's like to live and love as a butch. The stories inside are all unique, but they strike a similar chord of being different and proud, tough and vulnerable, handsome and beautiful.

Like all stories, we tell them for ourselves, so we can remember who we are and how hard we fought to get here. We also share our stories to blaze a trail for those who will follow in our footsteps. We took this path right here, we say, and we walked it with our heads held high and our eyes focused on the future. We walked it with swagger.

So, all hail the brave and beautiful butches, and if you're new around here, welcome, welcome, welcome.

~Rae Theodore

Table of Contents:

Pg 1 - Gender by Ash

Pg 2 - Butch Style 1950's—A Hersory by Merril Mushroom

Pg 6 - Intrinsically Butch by Faith Mosley

Pg 10 - Elaborations on a Hypothetical Butch Survey by Gwendolyn Bikis

Pg 17 - Watchful by Mary Cronin

Pg 18 - Becoming Butch by Georgie Orion

Pg 28 - Homage to the Dykes of My Youth by Abby Cohen

Pg 30 - Growing Up Butch in the Eighties by Cerys Meredith

Pg 31 - The Practice of Being Butch by Virginia Black

Pg 35 - City Butch by Cindy Rizzo

Pg 40 - Don't Tone It Down by Victoria Anne Darling

Pg 43 - The Butch Expectation by K. Aten

Pg 49 - Butch Is by Giovanna Capone

Pg 52 - Separations by Giovanna Capone

Pg 54 - To Have and To Be by Susan Spilecki

Pg 57 - On Being A Disabled, Butch Historian or: Not Walking With Two Ghosts by Steph Ban

Pg 64 - Clearly I Am Butch by Zeeb

Pg 66 - Why Did It Take So Long by Susan Silvermarie

Pg 69 - From Dad's Shirt to a 15-Foot Closet by John Dominic

Pg 78 - Rapture by Rowan Harvey

Pg 80 - When I Met Haruka by M. A. Dubbs

Pg 82 - Possibility by Claudia R. Asch

Pg 83 - Post Pandemic Butch Dream by Claudia R. Asch

Pg 84 - Butchness - A Compass by S.E. Smyth

Pg 92 - Authentically Butch by Gabby Cohen

Pg 94- Butch 4 Butch by Beck Guerra Carter

Pg 95 - On Being A Butch Creator by Missouri Vaun

Pg 99 - Summer Solstice Sunsets by Jen T. Stoughton

Pg 102 - Butch by Rebecca Ritts

Pg 104 - Quaintly Queer by Kristin Schloemer

Pg 109 - An Insider's Guide on How to Properly Appreciate a Butch by Rae Theodore

Pg 111 - Before the Slumber Party by Xequina Ma. Berber

Pg 120 - Bruised by JD Voss

Pg 127 - Being Me by Quay Zee

Pg 130 - On the Politics of Erasure by Giovanna Capone

Pg 132 - Definitions by Giovanna Capone

Pg 134 - Butch Is a Medium by Leander

Pg 136 - My Story of the Very Beginning by James

Pg 141 - Forgiving Seeds by Calliope Rose

Pg 145 - The Man My Father Made Me by Orlando Silver

Author Biographies

Gender by Ash

Butch Style 1950's – A Herstory
By Merril Mushroom

1950's glossary:

Soft butch – also known as butch on the streets, femme on the sheets.

Strict butch – dyke who insistently maintains the butch role at all times and who goes with femmes only.

Drag butch – butch who dresses and acts according to the male role stereotype and who often passes as a man in various aspects of her life.

Stone butch – a butch who does not let her partner touch her sexually.

Femmie-looking butch – any type of butch who looks enough like a femme to be mistaken for one or could even pass as a straight woman but self-defines as butch and behaves like a butch.

When I came out in the 1950's, role definition among my lesbian friends was a serious matter. Butch femme roles were important and clear-cut—otherwise, how would someone know who she could go with? There was even a category for lesbians who could be either butch *or* femme, or both. They were labeled ki-ki. Ki-ki lesbians were looked upon with some disdain by those of us butches whose role behavior never wavered, but they actually had the best of all worlds, since they could go with whomever they pleased. I knew butches who were really hot for one another, but they couldn't get it on, because one would then be derided for *flipping femme*.

The word butch can be a noun or an adjective. It could

be a statement of identity or could describe a particular set of behaviors and characteristics. My butch *self* is something I was born with, a sense of being that is more than learned behaviors or social categories. My butch *persona* is how I present to the rest of the world—at least the gay world. It was too dangerous to present as a butch to the straight world in those days when homosexuality was against the law and could be punished with incarceration. Still, many butches kept to their images wherever they were.

By and large, butch fashion, that is, appearance and mannerisms, fell into three main categories—greaser, sporty, and professional—and was primarily a matter of dress, hair, and behavior. Greasers wore their hair Elvis style and carried their cigarette packs rolled up in the sleeves of their T-shirts. Sportys were clean-cut, outdoor, athletic types, or they also could be cowboy types. Professional dykes who had to be very closeted tended toward tailored women's suits, shirtwaist dresses, hose and heels. They wore makeup and usually wore their hair long, but when they came out to the bars or parties, they often reverted to greaser or sporty and stuffed their hair into caps.

If I was in the mood, especially when doing the bar scene, I would go in full drag. I wore men's pants and shirts all the time anyhow, because I was very tall and they fit me better. I'd add a jacket to hide my breasts, since I was uncomfortable about binding them the way some of the other drag dykes did. I'd slick my short hair into a duck's ass with wing sides and a pompadour front, with one casual curl hanging just-so over my forehead. I was not wanting to actually *be* a man—just to *pass* as one. The whole point to doing drag was in the passing and the theatrics. Most butches I knew did not want to be men. What we really wanted were the goodies that men got. The power, the freedom, the pride, the paycheck, and the legitimacy and safety to be seen in public with the women we loved.

Straight men were known to beat up butches they saw on the streets.

The problem back then was that the only models we

had for our relationships were those of the traditional female-male heterosexual dyad, and we were too busy trying to survive in a hostile world to have time to create new roles for ourselves.

Women in the 1950's were considered to be incompetent creatures who depended on a man and were supposed to be faithful and subservient to husbands, children, and community. We definitely were not supposed to express any sexuality. As lesbians, we dared to go against all of that, and so we were social outcasts. Because we did not have any strong lesbian role models, we patterned our self-images and our relationships after those which were available to us. Maleness was equated with control, pride, and freedom. Femaleness was equated with weakness, dependence, and obedience. Female images often were used by the media in ways that were shameful and degrading. This was the pattern of the traditional heteropatriarchal expression of the day, and there was not yet a new feminist movement to expose it for what it was. So we, as butches, took on the male persona as the acceptable way to express our butch identity, but this actually had less to do with identity than with what we wanted to be our place in the world.

The basic dynamics of butch femme relating involve power, trust, vulnerability, tenderness, and caring. When I demand of my lover "Give it to me, baby. Now!" and she completely releases herself, flows out to me, I am so overwhelmed by the strength and the depth of her trusting me to hold her, keep her safe, and then give her back to herself. While she is freed to give herself up with no fear of getting lost, I can only do as she expects and hold her, keep her safe, and then give her back to herself.

The theatre part of being butch held great appeal for my friends and me. Along with the care we took with our dress and hair, we developed our butch swagger, practiced with and critiqued each other as to our stance, how we sat, the toss of our heads, movements of our shoulders. We became adept at holding our cigarette just so, pulling our zippo lighter out of our jeans pocket and running the wheel along the material of the leg, so we could present a ready flame to the cigarette of a femme. We were cognizant of our appearance at the pool table and the jukebox, of our performance on the dance floor where we always led and knew just how closely we could hold any partner. The way we combed our hair in public was as much a choreographed event as the way we danced or the way we played pool. We were fun to be with, and we were considerate, passionate lovers.

Style changed as the years went by. In the 1970's, when feminism educated us about different ways of viewing the world and defining ourselves, many dykes distanced themselves from role definition and butch behavior, insisted that there was no such thing as butch or femme. We wore jeans and flannel shirts, grew our hair long, or shaved it all off, or wore it any which way in between. But in my own secret mind, I still saw subtle—and sometimes not so subtle—manifestations of butch and femme in the dykes I knew.

In the 1980's, I became a land dyke. We country dykes all were strong, capable, assertive. We displayed and reveled in our power, and we did it without needing to identify with any male model. We may have given up most of the theatre around being butch, but in the world of the sisterhood of country dykes, we really didn't have time for that. Our basic identities might remain constant, but our behavior was focused on the demanding day-to-day tasks of our land dyke lives.

Now I am a very old dyke, and I haven't engaged in style, fashion, or theatre for many years. Well, maybe just a little... My body lets me know its limits in no uncertain terms, and perhaps my swagger has become more of a hobble. But over time and through many changes, the one thing of which I remain very sure is:

I am still the butch.

Intrinsically Butch
By Faith Mosley

Black. Butch. Lesbian. I'm not gonna lie—being mis-identified every single day for decades has taken a toll on me. I'm fifty-five years old, five feet nine inches tall, and about one hundred sixty pounds. I wear my salt and pepper natural hair short. My eyes are tired, but when I smile, I'm told I lose a decade. When I speak, I would think that the *sir* directed at me would immediately become a *ma'am* punctuated with an *excuse me* or even an *I'm sorry* accompanied by an apologetic smile, but no. That is never what happens. I'm sirred, and I speak, and the restaurant server or bank teller or receptionist or nurse or…just keeps on talking as though mine is a natural male voice when it isn't. It's not especially high, but it's distinctly female in register. I guess that the individuals misidentifying me have committed to their perception of what a man looks like so wholeheartedly that even my smile cannot shake the illusion.

I did not self-identify as anything other than lesbian until age twenty-three, when I lived in Iowa City, Iowa. I was headed to a gathering of gays and lesbians in a beautiful field that I'm sure no longer exists. This was thirty years ago and even hungry developers have discovered Iowa City. But back in the day, I strolled leisurely to a field in my jeans and T-shirt, a black woman relaxed. Just walking. Can you imagine? I'm sure it was a pride event, so I felt happy and included even though I was probably one of three other black lesbians in attendance. A woman who I would date months in the future sidled up to me and made some cheeky remark. I just shrugged my shoulders because I didn't know what to say in response to her flirtatious jibing, and she said, "You're so butch." What did

I feel at that moment? I felt a sense of rightness, and I smiled. Butch.

There was that word that immediately conjures up an image of Marlon Brando in *The Wild One* sitting astride his motorcycle with a leather jacket and a cap cocked to one side. Tough. Capable. Fearless. These are words that, to me, are synonymous with the word butch.

I was most certainly a butch kid— what in the old world— we called a tomboy. Why did we have to let go of that word? It was such a useful category for so many young girls who passed through that high action, more hunter than gatherer stage of young life development. Before breasts and periods, girls could be free from societal demands of femininity. I was a rough and tumble kid who wrestled my older brother and any kid in my neighborhood. I loved wiffle ball, basketball, soccer, and any kind of trouble I could find. I refused dresses or any type of frilliness thrust upon me. I was a child who cried if forced into a dress. This was a traumatic experience for me.

I did not know that my life was problematic until one day in 1977 when I was ten. I accompanied my mother to the mall and was dropped off at the Kinney Shoe Store and told that I could pick out my own shoes. My mom left to do her thing, and when she returned, I proudly showed off the beautiful tan hiking boots with the red laces—you know the ones. They're gorgeous and scream *Outdoor Ready!* The shoe salesman was beaming, equally proud because my long, narrow feet are hard to fit. *Too masculine.* That was all my mother said.

We left the store without the boots. Fast forward forty-five years. My fashion sense has barely changed, and I own two pairs of hiking boots. Tough, capable, fearless. Fearless. Unlike the Hollywood version that includes stoic, death-defying feats, my definition actually means scared shitless but I do it anyway. Many femmes I know are also tough, capable, and fearless…the difference being if and when they emerged from the tomboy stage, they evolved into feminine women who feel their power in their femininity. I, on the other hand, embraced my masculinity, albeit in a female body, and swaggering down the street in my Levis and flannel shirt —wardrobe stereotype I know, but very true for my Midwestern self— made me feel powerful, not weird or out of place. Of course, not all girls had tomboy stages, but for those of us who did, I think we mostly look back on those years with fondness, maybe even a few moist eyes. Puberty assaults us or eases into our unsuspecting bodies, and we change. Bodies change. Desires change.

So many butches, so many ways of being. Calling myself butch means I embrace the masculinity that for me has been one of many organic features that make me Faith. It is not a performance or a costume. It is simply the way woman/lesbian manifested for me. I have been a masculine person my entire life, and it has never conflicted with my female body. That's the beautiful part about being a human. We're nuanced creatures. Walking mosaics.

In the 1958 classic *Thunder Road*, I watched Robert Mitchum defy authority and run moonshine across state lines as his muscle car tore through primitive southern roads, and I remember sitting up and saying, *That's me!* I didn't mean I'm a white male outlaw. I meant his virility and F you to authority and his personal power resonated within my young mind and body. We were the same. I felt the same way when I watched *Lillies of the Field*. Sidney Poitier charmed his way into the lives of a bunch of nuns living in the Arizona desert. He helped them build a church. He was handsome, smart, funny, powerful, and vulnerable, too, being black in an American desert in 1963. *That's me!* It didn't matter that he was a man. We were the same. And black. And vulnerable, too. Vulnerable to so many preconceived ideas that people like to foist upon other people they don't understand or have never met. And then came *Gloria* starring Gena Rowlands. The 1980 crime thriller directed by her husband John Cassavetes. I was thirteen when I recognized the toughest woman on screen I had ever seen. Gloria was pretty and wore designer clothes. She was feminine and tough, capable, and fearless. She had two apartments in NYC, a lotta cash, and a gun. She knew how to handle herself. She operated outside the matrix. Powerful. *That's me!* Of course that was not me. None of those characters were me, but I admired their personal power and their ability to thwart the status quo and be who they were. Fearless. All three of these characters were role models for my developing butch psyche.

I think the word butch will always conjure up an image for most folks older than a certain age regardless of their sexual orientation. But the butch lesbian—the real-life masculine woman— has all but been symbolically annihilated in this modern, digital, brand-obsessed world. Yes, our brand is unmistakable, but we're hard to market, and sadly, survival in modern life requires buying into a marketing script that reads— women equals feminine, men equals masculine. People get nervous when you toss the script and be yourself. Mosaic. The nature of being a human is being nuanced. I liken it to the Ayurvedic doshas where one dominates, and maybe you're a Vata and those traits dominate, but the other two, Kapha and Pitta, also exist within you but to lesser degrees. I am routinely mistaken for a man because people are not used to the idea of masculine women even though we're everywhere, and even your grandparents have seen us.

My essence is butch. Essence is defined by Oxford Languages as "the intrinsic nature or indispensable quality of something, especially something abstract, that determines its character." Being butch speaks to an inner natural quality that I possess that was evident to some before I had a name for it. My essence lives deep within but reveals itself in how I walk, think, and dress. I've thankfully never battled my organic self. I was a butch kid who grew into a butch lesbian. I feel blessed despite decades of *sir, can I help you?,* and being screamed at and shooed out of countless women's restrooms. Here I stand, tough, capable, fearless, masculine woman. Intrinsically butch.

Elaborations on a Hypothetical Butch Survey
By Gwendolyn Bikis

When did you realize you were a lesbian?

Typically of me and my cautious Capricorn self, I'd made a decision about my future before I knew I'd made it. I was in high school, the year before my graduation. The spur was a short article, and a single picture. The article, "In Amerika They Call Us Dykes," lurked inside my friend Cathy's copy of *Our Bodies, Ourselves.* Amerika's photo absolutely arrested me— a group of white women, all cuddled up together, some, those I most closely examined, dressed mannishly. My first feeling was desire. It was, *I want to be like that.* The K in Amerika, I knew, signified that becoming like those women I was admiring would put me in a new, challenging, and different relationship with my country. In Amerika was my first small sign of the direction in which my budding butchness was heading.

When and where did you grow up?

I spent my adolescence, through the early seventies, in Baltimore County, not too far outside a town known as, believe it or not, Cockeysville.

Have you ever experienced street violence? Do you have an example?

Yes, one morning, a bad male driver nearly ran me over. In response to my angry, admittedly curse-laden reaction, he jumped out of his car to chase me with a tire iron. I bicycled away faster than he could run.

Have you ever experienced workplace discrimination?

Have many people underestimated your obvious

intelligence?

Yes and Yes.

Were you bullied growing up?

Yes. Name-calling, insults. I was allowed to know that I wasn't stacking up to Whatever Men Want. Yet, all the secret crushes I carried were for women. Or probably they weren't so secret. I used to dream, long past my adolescence, of walking though junior high school corridors, completely naked in front of everybody. In my waking adolescence, looking back, it seems that everybody knew but me. I was a lesbian, more obviously because I am a butch.

Notably, one of my best friends came out around as lesbian the same time as I did. Actually, maybe a little bit before I did. Yet, not being a butch, she has largely passed beneath the radar. Some femme lesbians, I know, decry this situation.

Have you ever been called aggressive when you were being assertive?

Yes. But this may be true for all women.

What do you typically wear, and not wear?

No, I don't wear a bra. I don't own one—and I'm not certain what happened to those I used to own. Each woman I have slept with, however, has worn one.

Yes, I own four leather jackets. A black leather motorcycle jacket. A black leather dress jacket that buttons, which a next-door neighbor, a Black man who raised three children by himself, informed me looked really good on me. Also a black leather jacket with a warm collar and warm cuffs made of thick wool-like fabric, that I bought inside a men's department, and a brown leather bomber jacket. For a butch, there are the chosen, and the unchosen garments.

So no, I never owned or wore a girdle. I currently own no dresses, skirts, robes, frills, nylon hose, or nightgowns. Some days, I wear men's underwear. Guess what? Men's garments are cheaper, better made, and last much longer. Butches know this.

One of my first cousins, gay and married to a man, is a year or two older than me. I remember the irony of looking through a Spiegel's catalogue with him. We paged through and chose, for each page spread, the garment we most longed to wear. While I chose the bulky, brass-buttoned coats and jackets, my cousin chose the coats that were more form-fitting, with long cuffs or cute little buttons that looked like seashells or small flat pieces of petrified rock.

Say yes to style without discomfort. The butch is not a chosen garment, it is who I am. Yet it's the butch in me that causes me to have my list of chosen garments. Yes to the backward Kangol. Yes, of course I learned to be my very best-dressed self from a femme who loves me. Bright ties, Italian loafers, a blue pin-striped zoot suit with tie and hat, and many Stacy Adams accoutrements. That would be shoes, ties, belts, pocket squares.

My favorite color is blue. I buy men's blue shoes. Most often blue tennis shoes.

No, I don't bind my breasts. And they are not sagging at all, unlike my mother's warnings of the disastrous *saggage* that would plague me if I refused to ever wear a bra.

I have no brothers, so I was surprised, the first time I saw my next-door neighbor Todd, as a four- or five-year-old, spray a bush with his hose. At the time, I thought it was kind of neat—even convenient. Yet I never thought to want my own hose, and now, I see it as more convenient that my clit and my vagina are more sheltered and safe in comparison.

Yet, yes, I have a dildo. It is lavender. Importantly to the core point of this essay, however, I did not choose this dildo by myself. I chose it with a femme. For butch is best achieved, maybe *only* achieved in concert with a femme. Although many straight women like and feel comfortable with me. Perhaps it is my helpfulness, and my home training. I try to be a gentle butch. Indeed, I remember the days when dykes used to talk about that type of woman known as a soft butch.

When and where did you come out?

I actually cashed in the promise that I made to my adolescent self when I came out in the eighties, in Boston. In my early twenties, I enjoyed a two-part coming out. First as a dyke, and then as a butch dyke. Importantly, I realized I was a butch *because femmes taught me.* I respect and I honor other butches, but *I fiend for femmes.*

The two women I have truly loved are both femmes. I loved to buy Lancome for my first femme, for the second, books.

Yes, of course I was a tomboy. No dolls, beyond a GI Joe. I had a cowboy outfit with bright metal cap guns inside a double holster. I played with racing cars, blocks, army men, plastic cowboys. I loved the books my Old-World, Latvian, Great-Aunt Vera gave me for Christmas but hated the skirts. They were woolen plaid, and itchy, and featured shoulder straps that felt binding to a girl butch who didn't want to wear their associated garment.

And yes, I played with boys, sometimes beating them up. I remember wanting to become a baseball player when I was in the third grade. My teacher, a young, new teacher, a white woman, urged me toward writing instead. So yes, I have written erotic butch femme fiction. Many thanks to two femme editors who first encouraged me— Joan Nestle and Lisa C. Moore.

And yes, I did play a sport. It was softball, another important stage in my nascent coming out. I played softball from the sixth grade until the eleventh. And the stories that are told and written about butches and team sports (See Lucy Jane Bledsoe) are true. Because, of course, throughout those years I developed several softball crushes, alongside the teacher crushes that cropped up frequently. The weeds of my desiring semi-consciousness. There were new ones each school year. In those years, I fell in crush with athletic femme women —all married. I Googled them— who played good softball and didn't throw like a girl, a huge disparagement shared between me and my sister.

How about hair?

Good question. I see a barber, press it with a cap when it's wet or unruly, lightly gel it in the morning. At the barber, I ask for number two clippers, and very short sideburns, for a cut that will be clean and trim all around my hairline.

In my childhood, my mother had my hair cut into a pixie style. One of my babysitters remarked that I looked like one of the Beatles. Still a child, I thought she meant a bug. Only once did my mother try pigtails on me. I hated the way they made me feel, and I hated the way my head hurt. I must've cried because she never again did that to me.

At twelve or thirteen, I received the social cues indicating that I was supposed to get rid of the hair on my body, but not on my head. For a while, I dutifully shaved and plucked. I tried to grow my hair long, but soon lost interest in *doing anything* with it. No perms, no styling, no nothing like that. Cutting it was a coming-out rite on par with the banishment of my bras.

Butch dyke is a very particular aesthetic, with a very peculiar appeal. The appeal is described perfectly in this passage provided by Jan Clausen.

"I'm watching Railroad Sue across the table. What I like, the small but clearly defined breasts, nipples darker circles under the clean white T-shirt…"

Sinking, Stealing, pp 191-193

Railroad Sue hops freights and wants to travel from Denver to Alaska. She is among The Brave and the Bold.

A few salient points about this passage. The first: Yay! Because my second and third points help to encapsulate butchness. That the erotic is contained in the tension, in one body, between the male and the female. Pert breasts, capable hands. Why is Railroad Sue so attractive? Because she is a woman who expresses maleness *in some ways*. She wears a white T-shirt, no bra, and a watch that usually men wear. But the frisson of butch attractiveness occurs in tantalizing combination— breasts, but no bra.

And the second, even more important point: butchness is expression-for-a-femme. The pull of this passage for me, a white butch, lies in its explained through the eyes of femme desire. A butch longs for its complement in the yin-yang dynamic of female relationships. A butch usually is defined by her desire for a femme—by delving into what a butch friend and I call the never-ending mystery of a femme.

Butches are among The Brave and the Bold. We play rugby, football, and basketball. We perform the electrical wiring of many buildings. We drive large city street cleaners and we speak up. When we think something is wrong, we may be the most likely people in America to say what needs to be said. I am, most times, the person in the room who says what everyone is thinking—which is the very thing that nobody wants to say. I have driven alone from Atlanta to Mississippi, through deeply rural routes, with books in my trunk whose contents constituted a chargeable offense from Batesville to Gulfport. Again, alone. "That's pretty daring," a friend of mine, straight and female, who travels a lot, sometimes alone and through the South, remarked to me. Yet, even more daring, I have a butch friend who drove across the country—again, by herself.

A butch will do all these things and more. Pet our animals, cook, sew, knit, decorate our houses, raise children and chickens, work as a clerk at the post office.

No, I *did not* spring from the pages of William Goyen's *Arcadio.* Butch is a lesbian woman who *expresses* herself, at times and in many ways, as the other gender—or equally as both. A butch does know what a tampon is. A butch may have a history of Modess use. A butch most likely knows cramps. I menstruated, menopaused, and even once was pregnant. Pre-lesbian, pre-diaphragm, I was the victim of a pink strawberry flavored rubber that ripped. Ovarian cycles, unenjoyable as they may be, are a part of the definition of butch womanhood. I wish many cramps on handily defeated California Gubernatorial Recall Republican candidate Caitlyn Jenner.

Butch is an authentic expression that sits firmly within a binary that is *real.* To use a model that is less Euro-centric than the one so rampant in these late stages of Caucasian American capitalism—a butch embodies, *as she is,* both gender ways, both social mores, of being. Of moving, talking, feeling inside a single body.

Being a butch requires balance. The butch is the blade—the very edge—of the double-bladed axe known as the labrys.

In Amerika, I am known as butch—it's a noun, or it's an adjective. Either way it's me.

References

Bledsoe, Lucy Jane: *Sweat;* Seal Press.
Clausen, Jan: *Sinking, Stealing;* The Crossing Press.
Nestle, Joan: *The Persistent Desire, A Femme-Butch Reader;* Alyson Books.
Moore, Lisa C.: *Does Your Mama Know; An Anthology of Black Lesbian Coming-Out   Stories;* RedBone Press.

Watchful
By Mary Cronin

Job Applicant, 1953

HELP WANTED-MALE

**Night Watchman-mechanically inclined.
steady work. 5-day week.
Mr. Spitz, Unity Hospital,
1545 St. John's Place.**

Sitting behind a desk
tapping on a typewriter,
tugging on my nylons?
That's no place for me.

Look here,
I've got my Navy WAVE training,
served as a parachute rigger
jumped out of a plane. That takes guts!

Watchful? That's me.
Working nights suits me fine.
And I can tinker and fix
good as any damn fella.

You wait, Mr. Spitz.
You won't find a better watchman
than me.

Want-Ad, "Night Watchman: Mechanically Inclined." *Brooklyn Daily Eagle,* 17 October 1953.

Becoming Butch
By Georgie Orion

Jo

A big yellow taxicab pulled into the driveway. Jo jumped out from behind the wheel with a soft grin on her face. She gestured for me to hop in and I did, sliding across the big bench seat, delighted by the expanse of it. This was so much better than our tiny hatchback. My mom threw a stack of giant buckets in the trunk before climbing in beside me. We were headed to the dunes. As we drove along, Jo and mom chatted and listened to the radio while I eagerly looked out the window, waiting for the beach to come into view. We spent the afternoon playing and picnicking in the dunes, with the Lake Michigan wind blowing through our hair. But, we were also there to work. I had a brand-new sandbox, after all, and we needed all the sand we could get. With glee, I used my tiny shovel to help mom and Jo fill bucket after bucket with our stolen hot white sand.

This is my earliest memory. I was three. It wasn't until many years later that I realized that Jo was a lesbian. It feels somehow significant that my earliest memory is of her. Her hair was short, dark, and wavy. She was shy and a bit awkward, but with kind eyes. Jo was around a lot during my early childhood. She took dance classes with my mom and ran in our city's annual 25k with my dad. But, it wasn't just Jo—it was Jo and Cecile, a package deal. With long brown hair, a thick French accent, and intense eyes, Cecile was Jo's polar opposite. Cecile wasn't unkind, but she was terse, with an air of confidence that I found intimidating even at a young age.

I don't know how old I was when I realized that Jo and Cecile weren't just friends, that they loved one another. Even though they were key characters in the story of my childhood, I don't recall Jo, Cecile, or my parents ever talking about their relationship in front of me until I was much older. Yet, I was drawn to them, so very curious—and yet, so very nervous about seeming too interested in them. But, I watched, hoping to learn more about these very interesting grownups and what their life was like.

As a teen, just as I was starting to understand who I was, I was awed by their relationship—a *long-term* lesbian relationship. And one that still lives on forty years after that day at the beach. With few role models of what it looked like to be coupled with another woman, I found solace in knowing that it could look normal…and last. More so, it was reassuring to see my parents have a long-term friendship with someone like Jo, someone like me. I hoped and prayed it meant that someday they would know the real me and that they would still love me.

Cash

Cash is the coolest butch I've ever known. A motorcycle mechanic and punk rock drummer today, at sixteen she rode a moped, played varsity basketball, and was the catcher on the softball team. Cash was nineties lesbian swagger personified. Despite being nothing like the other popular girls, she managed to live among them. And damn if they didn't adore her. Four years my elder, from my middle school vantage point, Cash appeared to have unlocked the secrets to the universe…or at least high school. One afternoon, she rolled up to one of my softball practices to umpire. By some stroke of luck, Cash recognized me. It turned out, Cash loved my mom. She had been in my mom's class in middle school and egged our house with a bunch of her friends. Feeling immense guilt, she turned herself in and, in doing so, managed also to endear herself to my mother. So, despite my inability to string together more than a few words as I donned my catcher's gear, Cash chatted with me at the plate. I left the practice on cloud nine with that kind of super-gay crush where you want to be that person, not sleep with them. I wanted her swagger. I wanted her moped. I wanted to look like her leaning up against the fence in a cutoff T-shirt with a flannel shirt tied around my waist.

In her last year of high school, Cash's older sister died tragically and unexpectedly, rocking our community. Cash graduated and immediately left the area. My mom managed to keep tabs on her, occasionally filling me in on stories that she'd hear through other teachers in the school. When I was eighteen, I came home from my first semester of college with a buzzcut, baggy jeans, and a wallet chain. Still not half as cool as Cash, but I was trying hard. Though I hadn't yet come out to my parents, my mom knew. While we did our holiday shopping, my mom filled me in on all of the things that had happened in my few months away at college, including the fact that Cash's parents had disowned her for being gay. My breath stuck in my chest. My face flushed. My heart pounded in my ears. I stopped in the middle of the mall unsure of what to say or do.

My mom turned, looked at me. "Is that what you are afraid of happening to you?"

I don't remember leaving the mall. It was all a blur. But somehow we ended up in the family van, driving around for what felt like hours. I sobbed. We talked. I'm pretty sure there was a McDonald's milkshake involved at some point. I was not kicked out. I was not disowned. I was maybe going to be ok. To this day, I feel gratitude for Cash paving my way to that moment. My guardian butch.

Years later, I was marching in the Chicago Pride Parade, and I thought I saw Cash in the crowd. For the rest of the day, I was obsessed with finding her. Was she even in Chicago? Could it have really been her? Would I even recognize her after all these years? Would she recognize me? I kept my eyes peeled as I wandered through the streets, hoping I'd find her and nervous about what would happen if I did. And then, like something out of the movies, the crowds parted and she was standing there. With her bright red hair worn in a ragged half mohawk/half mullet and head-to-toe tattoos, she looked like magic. Mustering the courage I never had as a kid, I flagged her down and told her who I was.

And she asked about my mom.

Cash was in a hurry, running off to a gig that night, so she invited me to see her band play at a bar in Wicker Park. That is how I ended up at my first punk show at the dirtiest bar I've ever been to in Chicago. Cash played the drums with an energy that lit me on fire. I thought she was cool in high school, but she had now transcended into some kind of queer, punk rock god. I was transfixed. Between sets, we drank beer and she introduced me to her girlfriend, a tall, leather clad high-femme with a punk-dominatrix vibe. After the show, Cash invited me to share a joint with her in the back alley, a gesture that made me feel seen and accepted in a way that I'd never been in high school. I partook, trying hard to hide the giddiness and nervousness coursing through me.

It has been more than twenty years since I walked out of the alley, and I've never seen Cash in person again.

The mythical punk-rock butch legend from my formative years, Cash remains the most badass human I've known. Knocking on fifty, she still rocks her buzzed red hair and an ever-growing collection of tattoos. A motorcycle mechanic and a bit of a vagrant, Cash lives a life wildly different from my own. Fortunately, she friended my mom, not surprisingly, and then me on social media, letting me continue to be a bit of a voyeur on her life, and living vicariously through her adventures. Cash still intimidates the shit out of me, but I am immensely grateful for the influence that she unknowingly had on my coming out and her small acts of kindness and acceptance during my baby butch years.

Sam

At thirteen, I felt like I was living someone else's life. With a mom who worked at the school, I didn't have the luxury of living one life at home and another at school. I colored in the lines. I earned straight As. I was an overachiever. Naturally lumped in with the other smart kids, I resented the identity and found that we had little in common other than our GPAs. I played sports. Good enough to make the team but not good enough to get much playing time, I was an accomplished bench warmer with a reputation for having a good team attitude. Coaches liked me, but I never really clicked with the other athletes. I secretly adored the skaters and goths, but they weren't too interested in me. They seemed suspicious when I sat with them at lunch as if I had been sent in as a spy. So I kept my head down and busted out my schoolwork, counting down to summer. Counting down to Girl Scout camp.

At Girl Scout camp, I belonged. The counselors were strong and funny and could do anything. They had strange names and wild hair. They wore cargo shorts and polo shirts and hiking boots. They had carabiners clipped to their belt loops, with keys that jangled as they walked. They smelled like campfire and sunshine. They sang with wild abandon and danced in the moonlight. They caught frogs and played in the mud. They noticed me and treated me like I mattered. I wanted nothing more than to be them, to be with them. I knew I had finally found my people. I didn't know at the time that I'd just discovered lesbians.

I had been attending Girl Scout camp since I was seven, but I was desperate to level up and join the ranks as a Counselor in Training. The CITs ruled the camp. Half camper, half counselor, they had just enough power without too much responsibility. Cursed with a late summer birthday, I was forced to spend one more year as a camper. I signed up for a two-week camp session that culminated in a multi-day canoeing trip. By some stroke of luck, our group was placed in the same unit of platform tents as the CITs. This was my chance. I might not be old enough to join them, but I was determined to befriend them. One person seemed to stand in my way. Sam fucking Baldwin. Two years my elder, Sam made me feel like I was a kid in a way no one else did. We both had blonde hair and blue eyes and lived in a baseball cap, but at six feet tall, she towered over me. We participated in other Girl Scout programs together and others noticed our similarities, calling me mini-Sam, making me simultaneously proud and resentful. There was something about the way Sam talked to me that made me feel there was a secret she was keeping from me. At thirteen, I wasn't sure what that was. But during the next couple years, I figured it out.

One weekend during the camp off-season, there was a call for volunteers to rebuild an Adirondack cabin on the camp's property. Always looking for any excuse to be among camp people, I signed up. This time, though, there were added bonuses. Chainsaws. Hatchets. Sam. I arrived early in the day, joining Sam's work crew. Despite the always present awkwardness between us, it was a glorious day. We donned our safety goggles, fell a few trees, notched logs, and rebuilt most of the three-sided structure. As we returned to the lodge that night, Sam joined a group of CITs and camp staff, sitting off in the corner chatting and laughing. Although we had a good day together, I was hesitant to follow her over. But Jess, one of the other CITs and Sam's closest friend, pulled out her guitar and started to play. It wasn't a camp song, but I recognized the tune. "Closer to Fine." What luck! My dad had unknowingly prepared me for this moment by introducing me to the Indigo Girls, Melissa Ethridge, and k.d. lang and teaching me three chords on the guitar. I had the perfect toolkit for befriending teenage lesbians. And especially Jess. Unbeknownst to me at the time, Jess was Sam's girlfriend and the key to breaking into the group and easing the awkwardness between me and Sam. I walked up to the circle and started singing along. Jess scootched over, making room for me to join the group.

It wasn't until more than a year later that Jess and Sam officially came out to me. And it took even longer before I came out to them. But, we had a mutual understanding—a don't ask, don't tell kind of agreement. They let me come out on my own time, but they indulged my questions and played tour guide during my late teens, gently sharing pieces of their world with me. They loaned me a copy of *Annie on my Mind*, my first sapphic novel. They brought me to my first queer bookstore. They accompanied me to my first gay bar, one that served lunch and dinner and didn't card before ten in the evening. Sam left for college when I was sixteen. Jess followed a year later. We wrote letters and met up when they were back in town for the holidays. During Thanksgiving break, I came out to Jess over a plate full of manicotti at Olive Garden. When I left for college the next year, Jess and I stayed connected online. We spent hours each night on ICQ and hanging out in queer chatrooms. Sam and I communicated less frequently, but she made the trip to Chicago to go to an Indigo Girls concert with me and became the first person to meet my first girlfriend. Sam was with me the first time I was accused of being a man in the women's bathroom. I was never as grateful for her six-foot imposing presence. She was my shelter and backbone.

When Sam and Jess broke up, Sam and I drifted apart. Jess had always been the glue that bound us together. Perhaps we never really had enough in common. Or maybe it was that we had too much in common. I'm not sure. Over the years, we've passed in and out of each other's lives. We've dated the same woman, had the same friends and the same mentors. In our forties now, we've both relocated to the same town more than five hundred miles away from where we grew up. We occasionally cross paths around town and at work. We seem to be forever caught in each other's orbit. For me, she is a time capsule, holding so many of the stories of my youth and a reminder of how far I've come.

A gaggle of butches

I was at Disney World when Ellen DeGeneres proclaimed *Yep, I'm Gay* on the cover of Time Magazine. I slipped away from my family one afternoon to walk to a gift shop and buy a copy of the magazine—a copy that I hid under my bed like it was porn, hoping it wouldn't be found. At that time, Disney had an Ellen-themed cafe with merchandise from Buy the Book, Ellen's workplace in the sitcom. Despite still being in the closet, I asked my mom to accompany me to the cafe to pick out a souvenir from our trip. I hoped that because we'd watched Ellen as a family, this request wouldn't seem too strange. My mom, who loved Ellen's comedy, and who surely was on to me at this point, gladly accepted my invitation. We drank coffee, ate giant rice crispy treats, and leisurely perused all of the Buy the Book merch. I walked out the door with an oversized Ellen coffee mug and a T-shirt.

I loved that T-shirt. It was the closest thing I had to gay pride gear in 1997. Wearing it felt empowering and terrifying at the same time. It affirmed who I knew I was, and I hoped it wouldn't seem overtly gay to my parents and everyone at school.

When I graduated from high school, my parents threw me a large graduation party. I wore that shirt. My parents invited all of their friends and our relatives. I invited lesbians.

Lesbians from Girl Scouts. Lesbians from camp. Lesbians from church. Lesbians from school. Basically every grown-up lesbian I had ever met. And they all showed up. There were more short haired, khaki and hiking-boot clad women at that party than my little butch heart could have hoped for. Of course, I hadn't come out to any of them. And none of them had ever actually come out to me. But they were the grownups who saw me, the grownups that made me feel normal. My secret village, my gaggle of butches. It was the highlight of graduating from high school.

Sorority girls and silver foxes

At seventeen, I barely had a toe out of the closet, but I was desperate to move away from home and attend college in a real city. A Midwest kid, Chicago seemed the place to go. Of course, not knowing anything about Chicago, I didn't consider the fact that not all parts of the city (and certainly not all universities) would be equally accepting or liberal. At a small private engineering school on the south side of Chicago, I felt like I was a million miles away from Boystown and Andersonville, the nearest queer meccas. My college campus was largely white, male, and conservative. I knew I needed to find a community of women to survive. I didn't expect that my community would turn out to be a sorority.

My first week of college, I attended a few rush events with women from my dorm. Although still firmly in the closet, I wore my Ellen T-shirt and had already plastered my dorm room walls with pictures of the Indigo Girls and Ani DiFranco and a particular girl from back home that I was secretly in love with. I hadn't yet shaved my head, but I certainly didn't look or act like a stereotypical sorority girl. Of course, neither did most of them. Although they were all straight, they were the kind of women that opted to go to a predominantly male technological university in the 90s. They were delightfully nerdy. And they were tough. The sorority officially invited me to pledge following a game of laser tag at the end of rush week. Three months later they inducted me as a member. I had recently shaved my head for the first time and was not-so-secretly sleeping with one of my sorority sister's roommates, so I knew that they knew exactly who they were bringing into their sisterhood. That was only the beginning.

During the seven years I spent in Chicago completing both my bachelor's and master's degrees, I only met a handful of other queer students at the university and most of them were men. Our Gay-Straight Alliance, as it was called back then, held secret meetings in unmarked locations. Despite having very few queer friends, my pack of fiercely supportive straight sorority sisters sustained me. They weren't simply supportive of who I was, they helped me discover what it meant to be queer and butch, accompanying me on adventures in the city that I wasn't brave enough, or foolish enough, to go on by myself. They were my entourage, escorting me to my first Chicago King's show, even helping me dress in drag myself—binding and applying facial hair, a thrilling and eye-opening experience. They brought me to a queer kiss-in on DePaul University's campus. It was an afternoon outing that turned into a multi-day mind- and life-altering excursion that introduced me to the north-side lesbian party scene, the Lesbian Avengers, and the joys of Jello wrestling. They accompanied me to Boystown to explore Gay-Mart and sex toy stores, even helping to coordinate with the staff at one store to host queer-friendly, sex-positive sex-ed sessions in the dorms. They attended pride parades. They decorated my car with a *Vermont or Bust* sign when I ran off with my college girlfriend to get a civil union over spring break. They were there for me when we split up a decade later.

But, out of everything they did for me, the most important adventure was when they accompanied me to the Lost and Found, one of Chicago's oldest, and now defunct, lesbian bars. We piled into a cab and were let out in front of a building that vaguely resembled the description that I'd read in an early online forum. As instructed, we knocked. A few moments later, the door opened and an older woman looked us up and down and then—perhaps a bit reluctantly—let us in. The bar was dark and smoky, and there were no more than ten patrons in the place, including us. Some played pool, others chatted at the bar. We ordered beers and sat down at a table, making idle conversation and trying not to look like tourists. I remember so little of what we did that night or what we talked about. But a few details remain crystal clear even two decades later. The alarm system to alert patrons in a raid. I knew about Stonewall and had read *Stone Butch Blues*, but to see this evidence of the realities of the not-so-distant past was sobering. I imagined what I would do in a raid and considered whether I was wearing clothing that would pass the checks in the sixties and seventies. I was not.

And tampons. The bathroom had a box of tampons under the sink. I'm not sure how I discovered this in the first place and why this detail has stuck in my memory for twenty years. Perhaps it was the fact that this signaled that the space was designed by women, for women. For women like me. For a butch like me.

What struck me more than anything, though, was the bartenders. They were the butchest dykes that I'd ever seen, and they were beautiful. I instantly fell in love with them. With sparkly silver hair, they radiated an intensity and power that I'd never before witnessed. They weren't exactly dapper, they certainly weren't wearing suits. But they were so authentically themselves. And they were old. I'd met some lesbians in their forties, maybe even their fifties, but these butches were the same age as my grandparents, not my parents. To see a person who looked like me—the me I wanted to be—but five decades older, was profound. Those enchanting silver foxes, my butch elders, created this space in a time where doing so was difficult and dangerous. I was humbled. I only spoke a few words to them that night, but when I close my eyes I can still see them leaning up against that bar and the slight head nod we exchanged across the room.

Fast Forward

I am forty-three now. I look in the mirror and see the faces of all of these butches looking back at me. The silver hair emerging around my own temples, making my fresh fade sparkle in the sunlight. The tailored suit jacket that I can finally afford. The crinkles around the corners of my eyes when I smile. Jo. Cash. Sam. The gaggle of butches at my graduation party. The silver foxes. I am nothing like them and everything like them. Their stories shaped my story. Their courage made me brave. Their attention made me feel seen. I spent my youth looking for idols, looking for another way to be. These butches gave me hope to build upon. They let me see them, so that I could start to see myself.

Homage to the Dykes of My Youth
By Abby Cohen

Dykes. Bull dykes. Diesel dykes. Pool sharks. Heavy smoking hard drinking heavy-set women in their jeans and flannel shirts and tight T-shirts and sagging tits and tattoos and swagger and a bottle of beer. They filled Sneakers night after night. Those women who had by God survived. And if you don't know what that means, go read up on your history because to say they survived is a miracle. There were so many fallen along the way.

I once talked to a woman who looked like some sort of throwback to that earlier era. She was too young to have been an adult with that beehive hairdo and that makeup. Why, I'll never know. But she told me her story of how the parents of her partner had the woman locked up in a mental institution, and I know it was the mid-eighties by then, but apparently where there's enough money there's a way. I don't know what became of them.

But let's hail the survivors. And remember the fallen gone too soon in a million different ways. In a world where the only way out was that bar full of smoke and booze, how many of those women of my memory died too soon from cancer or got lost inside a bottle. Hail those of us who survived. We're still here and though I haven't gone to a gay bar in years, I'm now feeling an urge to dig out a pair of black ankle boots—I had several different pairs—and polish them up and swagger up to the pool table. They've closed down the Toasted Walnut, sadly. The owner has cancer and couldn't cope, even without a pandemic. So Philly's without a women's bar. Again. Who knows if we'll have another? And certainly nothing like the dive that was Sneakers. Or the Lark, a gay bar for both genders. What is there about a dive that speaks to me in a way those shiny latter-day discos never did? Some part of me that must be a reincarnation of a working-class queer that drove a cab or ran an elevator. Well, maybe not. But either way, let's just pause for a moment to remember the women who held their ground in their heavy boots and their black high tops and never allowed anyone to make them into anything but their unapologetically bull dyke selves.

Growing Up Butch In The Eighties
By Cerys Meredith

Tomboy. Baby Butch. Wild child. Half a boy. No skirts for me, thank you very much. The long hair gets in the way. Keeps catching on to the branches of the trees and is full of sand all the time. I used to have pipe curls. Yeah, very cute. Combing it? Torture. Can I have short hair? I was very proud of my eighty's mullet. I still am.

Garcon manqueé is what my Gran used to call me. A missed boy, the French dictionary tells me. The boy that's unfinished. Rolled off the line too early. Oops, sorry. That one got away.

Garcon manqueé.

My Gran used to say that with such a loving undertone and warmth in her eyes, so I didn't really mind.

I still turn to that warmth whenever I need it and it still manages to calm me down. Bless her.

The Practice of Being Butch
By Virginia Black

"If you will practice being fictional for a while, you will understand that fictional characters are sometimes more real than people with bodies and heartbeats."—*Richard Bach, Illusions: The Adventures of a Reluctant Messiah*

I was butch before I knew what the hell it meant, before I knew I was queer.

It was tomboyish at first, back when I was a teen and thought myself boy-crazy. Later, I realized I wanted to *be* the boys I was following around, and though I was down for a kiss or three, not one of them was going to actually get in my pants.

I grew up a Gen X kid in a large city. My pop culture world and therefore the framework of my life was defined by what I saw on *MTV* and during primetime television. Some of those images were more captivating than others and planted the seeds of the kind of woman I wanted to be.

The Eurythmics' Annie Lennox and her masculine suit in the video for "Sweet Dreams" was interesting, yes, but I couldn't emulate that on a poor kid's inconsistent allowance. Judas Priest's Rob Halford, however, and his gritty leather heavy metal posturing had the game I wanted, and I could pull off that look with ripped-up jeans and a black T-shirt.

Jo, the swaggering, motorcycle-riding tomboy on *The Facts of Life* was compelling, sure, and my obsession with her was a huge hint about my identity, but I didn't want to be her. Instead, I wondered what was interesting enough about the characters of Steve Trevor and Steve Austin to attract Diana Prince, *Wonder Woman*, and Jamie Sommers, *The Bionic Woman.*

I didn't want to be those women, either, but I wanted to get their attention.

By 1986, I had the queer part figured out, but then things got even more convoluted. One wasn't just gay—what kind of gay? Defining oneself was required, particularly if one actually wanted to get laid, which I did. That meant I had to be in the right place, looking and acting like I belonged—requiring more emulation and attempted execution.

Butch was supposedly phasing out in the 1980s, but that was utter bullshit. The women I went to college with who claimed butch/femme was an outdated dynamic, though half of them had short hair, chewed tobacco and played softball, had obviously not been in a bar recently, and if I wanted to get lucky, I had to choose.

My choices at the time were limited based on my environs and minuscule experience. Granola-eating lesbian or softball dyke? Neither fit, so I kept looking, but butch as a label didn't seem accurate. The books I read—and I read everything with lesbians in it that I could get my hands on, which at the time wasn't much—were supposed to help define me but didn't. I read them all, trying to find myself, but I wasn't there.

Instead, they helped me rule out the kind of butch traits I didn't want to have. I have never bound my breasts. I have never passed as a man. I have never played team sports. At least, I don't remember having ever played, which may mean I played and it was so traumatic, I blocked it out. I didn't downplay whatever supposedly feminine traits I enjoyed, and I was never, ever in a million years going to be the kind of dyke who didn't want to be sexually penetrated, like some of the women in those books.

I picked and chose what I could from the sources I could find and acted like the fictional characters I read or saw on television or in films. I emulated the other women in the bars I snuck into before I was of legal age, like the bartender who wore spurs on her boots and cranked Melissa Etheridge's first album to maximum volume. I thought it was infatuation, but it turned out I wasn't so much crushed out on her as I wanted to be her.

And then there were the sources I didn't realize had shaped me until much, much later. I walk and smoke, when I rarely partake, like my stepfather. I hated him so much when I was a teen, but the moment I was on my own out in the world, his advice was what I followed the most, his arrogant distrust of a white-run world was what I carried with me into the bars where only two or three black women lurked in the corners.

Enter *Vanity Fair* magazine and k.d. lang's famous shave from Cindy Crawford on the August 1993 cover, and suddenly the game changed. After a brief, possibly misguided phase that included boot-cut black Wranglers and roper belts, I leaned more toward a more gentlemanly butch, the chivalrous dyke. Ties never quite fell right across my chest, but suit jackets and dress shirts took over my life and never left.

Around the same time, my identity experienced a seismic shift as my burgeoning taste in BDSM and the world of leather led me to a whole new community of butch women. These women, many of them tops, showed me how to hold my own space, regardless of expectation or what other people around me were doing. I learned how to move so people got out of my way. I learned how to speak so people paid attention.

I learned why Rob Halford had fascinated me in the first place, and it wasn't just the leather pants. When the boots changed from cowboy to biker, I felt like *me*. After that, I walked into most spaces saying, *this is who I am* instead of *do I belong here?,* and it saved my sanity.

I learned that practicing to be someone else didn't hold as much value as I'd thought.

While I have emulated men and masculine presentation, I have never wanted to be one, nor felt the need to defend my space as a lesbian against a man…unless he was trying to manspread on public transportation, so I did it first to prove a point. How straight men perceive me doesn't shape my self-definition.

That definition is about butch presentation, not necessarily butch competency. Though I've proudly worn flannel, I suck at chopping firewood. I haven't attempted to fix a car since I was twenty-two. Spoiler— it did not go well. My wife handles the power tools, though she's closer to the femme end of the dynamic, but when we go out, I'm the one with boots on and a multitool somewhere in my pockets, and she's wearing the lipstick.

I'll die on this hill, I can't be butch without the contrast of femme. If I'm butch, femmes define me. Feeling dapper in a suit is only complemented by the woman on my arm, the one who sees me for who I am. I can only feel suave opening the door if the woman I invite before me understands the gesture for the compliment it is—I care about your comfort, your enjoyment, your pleasure before mine.

The walk I perfected in those biker boots meant so much more when a smiling femme yelled *nice stroll* through her car window. I have never been attracted to another butch. Fictional ones, maybe. But even fictional butches are a tad on the femme side—*Battlestar Galactica*'s Starbuck, or anything with Michelle Rodriguez.

Hell, I didn't even see a black butch that came close to who I am or who I always wanted to be until I saw Lea Robinson walk across my screen in an episode of the recently remade *A League of Their Own, the* 2022 version. My jaw dropped. Bertie, a trans man, held space, dressed, and acted in a way so familiar to me, I barely tracked the rest of the plot…but even that man didn't hold all the parts of my ideal, of what kind of butch dyke I want to be.

Nearly forty years since the journey began, I continue to pull together the pieces of that definition. Years—it took me *years* to learn that I didn't need to find a place where I fit. Instead, I needed to mold the world around me as I am, a boot-strolling, suit-jacket wearing, whiskey drinking, red-blooded Black American dyke, trademark pending.

To be fair, I'm still learning. One day, though, I found myself walking down a street, moving through the world as myself, no longer focused on the *practice* of presentation, of *becoming* something or someone else.

The best part about being butch is the way I feel when I hold my space. The way I walk, talk, drink, make love—all these things are second nature to me now after decades of practice, of finding how I want to fit in the world.

The hardest? The constant second-guessing when I'm in a new space, questioning if those around me see what I want them to see. This concern might be mine alone and not indicative of the overall butch experience, but it is endless. I wonder if I will ever *not* consider how some others perceive my butchness.

I no longer, however, seek their input, so…how do I define my butchness now?

Exhale.

However I want.

City Butch
By Cindy Rizzo

I entered the restaurant, and they were all there—the people from my butch-femme mailing list, FABU-east, femmes and butches united. Like characters out of a novel come to life.

I looked around at the butches congregated at the front. My first thought—*I need to buy a leather jacket.*

I smiled and practically laughed out loud when a butch I said hi to responded with, *hey bud,* a greeting that up until that moment had only lived in email. They really talk like that, I thought, almost giddy with excitement.

Jay and Joe and Jude and Sunny and Akiva and Kooch. I had no idea who was using their screen names and who was using their real names, though I suspected Kooch's birth certificate likely said something else. I had one of the most female names, though I never thought about introducing myself as anything other than Cindy. Some of them knew me as Boston Butch, a screen name I used. But I was fine with Cindy or Boston or even Bud.

FABU-east was one of a number of geo-focused discussion email lists. All of the FABUs were all off-shoots of the butch-femme.com website, a community space with pre-Instagram picture sharing and lively, topical forums that sometimes descended into warfare, but were mostly innocuous. *What Did You Have For Dinner Tonight?* was one of the most popular.

When we were seated, it was at a long, rectangular table which gave me a good look at the group. I'd already chatted up the butches while we waited. But now I could feast my eyes on the femmes.

I'd come into my own butch identity a while back in a past relationship, having been a studious follower of Joan Nestle's 1980s writings, reviving the butch-femme dynamic from its Second Wave feminist dismissal as role playing and the dreaded hetero-patriarchy. But Joan, and all those who followed with powerful, assertive writings, saw great value in the strength, the loving vulnerability and the transgressive self-definition of butch-femme identities. We weren't imitating or perpetuating the straight world. We were reshaping and transforming it into something much more authentic and much less limiting. Femmes could be celebrated for their ability to fix a carburetor or assemble some crazy cabinet purchased from IKEA. Butches could get flustered and tongue-tied at the sight of a beautiful femme or be frustratingly unaware of a femme's blatant flirting, also known as the two-by-four butch.

It was all part of what we called The Dance.

While there was much more leeway and flexibility within a butch identity than there was for real men in the straight world, I still at times worried back then whether I could be considered a real butch. My longing for a black leather jacket instead of my tired, cloth winter coat was an example of that. Could I really fit in if I wasn't wearing the prescribed clothing like everyone else? Did it matter that I wasn't mechanically inclined and would rather have been reading a book than change the oil in my car? Was I a city butch? An intellectual butch? How far could I stray from a stereotype so I could be true to myself?

While those insecurities bothered me, I knew in spite of everything that I was a butch. It was clear to me from my awestruck reaction when a femme got all dressed up for a special occasion. To this day I still smile when my femme wife rolls her eyes after I'm unable to answer whether she should keep or return a skirt she just bought. I get a hug and a thank you when I fix whatever computer or iPhone problem she's having. And when it comes to opening a stubborn jar… Well, sometimes I'm successful and sometimes it's her.

My interest and attention will always be focused on the girly girls, especially the ones who have some meat on their bones. I'm a bit more partial to blondes and the smart ones. The ones who care about the state of the world are the ones who rock mine. That's why I married one.

Of course, I can appreciate another butch. Lea DeLaria is funny and outrageous. Wanda Sykes is hysterical. Rachel Maddow is brilliant. Queen Latifah is an amazing performer. Alison Bechtel is talented beyond measure. Brittney Griner is a great athlete—who should be free, by the way. But my awe and appreciation of other butches is more of the head-nodding, fist in the air, *yeah* variety as opposed to the dry-mouthed, stomach-clenching, rapid heart beating type.

Maybe that's how I'm sure about what I am. Or maybe the fact that ever since I can remember, and the first of those memories goes back to age five in kindergarten, I hated wearing dresses and skirts and carrying a purse. Or pocketbook as we used to say. I went to school at a time in the early 1960s when girls were forbidden to wear pants. So, without pockets for my stuff, I had to carry something to hold whatever I needed. This was before we all wore backpacks or carried messenger bags. Instead, there was the purse, which I constantly forgot to take with me, leaving it in my school desk or hanging on the back of my chair on many occasions.

When the dress codes in NYC public schools changed and I could wear jeans in seventh grade, it was like a weight had been lifted from my shoulders. I could be me with my house keys in my left pocket, my wallet in my right. Same arrangement as today.

In those more counter-cultural, Woodstock-era days, most girls I knew wore long jeans, frayed at the bottom because they dragged on the ground, T-shirts and sneakers or work boots. We shopped at the Army-Navy store and wore denim work shirts over our T-shirts.

When the fashions changed, I never did. I still wear jeans and button-down shirts, mostly purchased from the men's department. My clothes now come from a combination of gendered stores—mostly men's shirts, women's jeans, shoes in both male and female sizes, and as many non-gendered clothing types as I can find. I dress up in vests and bow ties, sometimes with a jacket. One measure of family acceptance came when my cousin gave me her father's bow tie collection. I was thrilled.

I've lived through a number of eras that have either vilified or celebrated the butch identity. I was a child when Joan Nestle and her sister femmes flirted with butches in gay bars in the 1950s and when Leslie Feinberg wrote about their early days as a butch in upstate New York. When I finally came of age, it was through Second Wave lesbian feminism and the pushback against butch-femme identity. Then Joan and others spoke up in the 1980s and I was able to acknowledge myself as a butch, which led me eventually to butch-femme.com, FABU-east, and my own femme girl.

These days, we hear a lot about the disappearance of butches in pieces titled something along the lines of *Where Have All the Butches Gone?* The argument is that butches are all becoming transmen, much to the chagrin of lesbian femmes. But as my friend, Roey Thorpe, a self-identified femme, wrote in response, those who've transitioned were always trans, often identifying as butch because in prior years there didn't seem to be an alternative to enabling them to be their authentic selves. Now there is, and instead of whining, we should be happy for them and for all of us who are able to understand more about ourselves and our own gender identities and gender expressions.

I've always felt that trans folx and non-binary or gender expansive folx make more room for all of us, especially butches. All those insecurities I once had that maybe I wasn't butch enough can now be laid to rest. Gender itself, we have learned, is a social construct, and it's fine to place yourself into an identity yet still pick and choose among your own interests and inclinations.

It's likely that now that I'm in my sixties, my gender identity as female is pretty secure. And my gender expression as butch, or masculine-of-center, also feels right. That's how I've begun to think about it.

It's possible that many butches at one time or another have thought about our gender identities. Am I trans? Do I think I'd be more authentically myself if I were to transition? There's nothing wrong with posing those questions, no matter who you are. It's actually a blessing that we are living at a time when we can feel okay about asking them.

For me, asking those questions has helped me clarify the difference between my gender identity and my gender expression. Maybe part of me is still influenced by coming of age in the dawning of feminism and lesbian feminism to still feel proud to call myself a woman and even to continue using female pronouns. Though I'm okay, really, with any pronouns. My wife calls me Mister Fish as in, as you wish, Mr. Fish. Don't ask.

But I understand and am happy that each person gets to decide these things for themselves—gender identity, gender expression, pronouns, all of it. I'm convinced, and hope others are as well, that at the heart of both feminism and LGBTQ activism is the vision that people should be able to live as their true selves, free from the bonds of hetero-patriarchy and white supremacy.

I did go out and buy that leather jacket, and I still put it on when the weather is cool but not yet cold. It makes me happy to wear it along with my jeans, my button down, and my always short hair. This is the me who I knew I was at age five when I was forced to wear a dress to school. It's the same me I was able to become so many years later. A city butch. An intellectual butch. A butch who still can't change the oil in her car, who can make a killer eggplant parm, who prefers the bed at a Westin to a sleeping bag in a tent, who loves politics and the news, who roots for the Mets and the Red Sox and yet knows nothing about the players or their stats. One who prefers beer but will still drink wine, who cried with Evelyn Hugo when Cecilia St. James died and when Theresa in *Stone Butch Blues* broke up with Jess, and who never again has to wear a dress or carry a pocketbook.

Don't Tone It Down
By Victoria Anne Darling

Countless times over the years
You have chosen to wear
Something less
Hard
Something less
Specific
Something less
Male

You've been told by
Trusted lovers
Frightened mothers
Concerned fathers
And even your closest friends
To dress
Less obvious
Less overt
Less masculine

Even without thinking
You've
Searched your closet
Questioning
Will this be
Too much
Too noticeable
Too butch

Are you crazy?

Did you know I scan
Grocery aisles
Theaters
Parking lots
Government lines

For someone like you

Each day is a new conflict waiting to face
How many will mistake my feminine for weakness
How many will reach out to touch what isn't theirs
How many will count me with the moral majority just because
of how I look

Seeing you in a crowd of strangers makes all the difference in
the world

Finally
Heart racing
Blush creeping
Breathing deepened

I'm
Alive
Sexier
More powerful

Less
Invisible
Less
Straight-seeming
Less
Wasted

Being able to see you means
I'm not alone
It's my proof
That I'm not one of them
Not
Made for a man
But rather
Made
For a butch

Please don't tone it down
Maybe we'll never meet and
I won't get you into my warm bed

Maybe we'll never be friends
Co-conspirators
Or confidants
But even so
You'll still be
My champion
Hero
Brave knight
My renegade pirate

In my dreams
And on the street
You make it worth
Being femme

So square your shoulders
Pull out your bad-boy-rough-trade self
Be that Dapper Dan you've kept hidden
Don your obviously male
And let the butchest part of you move up to
Start riding in the front seat

Don't tone it down –

So that I
And others like me
Can
Find you
Love you
Sex you
Drink from you
Whether you know
We're watching
Or not

No matter what you do

Don't, don't, *don't*
Tone it down.

The Butch Expectation
By K. Aten

No one ever called me pretty except old adults. I've been told I was cute on a few occasions, but it wasn't something I expected to hear or heard often. I was too fat or too weird until the time in my early twenties when I became a gym rat and I wasn't either of those things. Even then, I was considered other by many. I had boyfriends, I had sex, and I most definitely had a dominant personality. But I wasn't butch. At least not until I came out. But I attest to this day that butch isn't an outward appearance as much as it is equal parts attitude and expectation.

Looking back, I had no idea what I was in my mid-twenties. I just knew something was missing and I wasn't finding it in my eight-year relationship with my fiancée. I discovered fan fiction, and love between women. I left behind friends, a job, and my hometown. Everything dropped away in my search of identity.

During this journey, lovers came and went. I came out again and again. But I constantly circled around the drain of personal discovery. It was a dirty, arduous, and sometimes heartbreaking process. Throughout it all, I was regarded as butch by people that didn't know me. The hilarity was that the friends that did know me simply shook their heads with a smile. Sure, I had short hair, a muscular build, and I liked to play sports. I was aggressive in the pursuit of winning, and definitely in charge while in pursuit of romance.

The truth is that I never felt butch. There was a void where my identity should be. I didn't feel feminine or masculine, I was just me. Despite all the outward signs, I'm also an intellectual, a poet, a deep thinker, and a book worm. I carry nail files wherever I go and frequently wore lip gloss. Covid and middle age has made me forgo lip gloss and eyeliner most of the time. I'm layered like an onion. I can't be sorted into the binary boxes of butch and femme, and I'm not the only one. But society is comfortable with binary, especially the elder generations of social freedom fighters. It's familiar and change is scary.

I'm going to tell you a story about my butch-ness. The year is 2003 and my then girlfriend talked me into a trip to Key West, Florida, specifically for Womenfest. It was the beginning of September and would also be an early celebration of my twenty-ninth birthday. Resorts had all-day poolside activities, there were street parties, and a lot of women. So many women. One particular day we were with a few of my girlfriend's friends and their large friend group. One woman was a deeply tanned, and very butch lothario, and vocal about it. Another had buzzed dark hair, similar to me in build and attitude. I wanted a new suit when I hit Key West and as such, wore the new one for the day. Me in a coral-colored bikini, can you imagine?

There were many events and much alcohol to be had throughout the day. Pairs of couples would go up on the stage and compete to see who could find the cherry hidden in whipped cream all over their partner's bodies, before swimming across the pool and delivering it into the hands of the drag queen judge.

There were only two bathrooms in the pool area of this resort, and lines were exactly as long as you could imagine in an at-capacity pool full of mostly women drinking in the hot sun. At one point I got up to go to the bathroom and the line was at least twenty long. But only for one bathroom. I asked what the issue was, out of toilet paper perhaps? No. Apparently the toilet was clogged. I asked if there was a plunger and everyone said yes. Seriously? Yes, I did my best Mario impression and took to the toilet with fury. I cleared the clog, did my business, and came out to applause. Why? Because I took one for the team and did my butch duty. I guess. Yeah, me in my coral bikini flexed a little muscle and told that teepee to move along.

Roughly an hour later, the last big event was due to start. The Beach Blanket Butch and Beach Blanket Babe competition wasn't a talent show, and wasn't based on appearance, but it was some sort of weird bastardization of both. Some of the women in our group urged a few of us to do it. I was hesitant because the night before there was a competition at a bar with leather, studs, and such. I wanted to enter with my leather vest on and I was told by my admittedly horrible girlfriend that I shouldn't because I would only lose and be embarrassed. I did enter because I was drunk, it looked fun, and I'm not letting anyone put me down. I also was the only woman winner. Granted, there weren't many but still. Anyway, her words hurt my confidence so I hesitated. The new friends wore me down. The butch lothario Dallas, yes, she was from Dallas, entered the butch contest. The other woman similar to me borrowed a coconut bikini top and entered the babe contest, which we all found hilarious. I was told to put on my cargo shorts to butch me up and go enter. I did.

The competition was simple. The babes only had to get in line and walk up and across the stage, do a little turn, then walk off. The butches had more to do. Perhaps that's the first indication of the expectation part of being butch, more work involved. Butches were required to put on a tool belt before walking onto the stage and giving their best pick up line to the crowd. I had suggestions flying at me from all the folks in our group. Say this or say that. This is my favorite pickup line…you get the point. With all this in my head, I made my way to the butch line and stood to wait my turn, going through all the possible things I could say in front of hundreds of people.

There were easily sixty folks in the long butch line. Some were so butch they were indistinguishable from the many men I used to work with in the factory north of my hometown. Bulging biceps, buzz cuts, and attitude rolling off them. Some people recognized me from the bathroom thing and cheered me in line, but I zoned out. I was nervous despite singing karaoke every weekend back home. I finally decided to warm up the crowd with an opener before going into the pickup line I'd settled on. It was a sure bet, right?

The woman before me sang to the crowd and they went absolutely wild. I should have sung something, I love karaoke. She wasn't that good but she was clearly a local and had so much enthusiasm. She was big, strong, and seemed butch. I had fears that I wasn't going to be butch enough. Then they fastened the belt around my waist and sent me on my way. Up the steps, and to the center of the stage where the announcer handed me the microphone. I looked out over the crowd and launched my warmup comment.

"They gave me this tool belt, but I'm afraid I left all my tools *wink* in my room." They loved it! I was riding high and I was ready to deliver my pickup line, I was—shit. I'd completely forgotten what I was going to say. I froze. Moments later, the announcer says, is that it?

Embarrassed, I gave her a wide-eyed stare and nodded. Then I thrust the microphone back at her and walked off the stage. The friend group cheered for me when I made it back to our chairs. Someone bought me a drink. It was fun despite the hiccup. Then they called back the top ten, based on initial judges' decision. Dallas and I both made it! I put my cargo shorts back on and went to line up across the stage with the rest.

As we're standing there, one very butch woman points at Dallas's toes and says, "You can't be butch. Your nails are painted." Another agreed with her. I looked down at my own toenails which were painted the bluest blue you can imagine. I asked her what was wrong with it and she called me out as well. The karaoke singer also spoke up in defense of painted toes. The ten butches on the stage quieted when the announcer called out to the crowd. The rest would be decided solely on crowd reaction. Judges would mark the top three winners based on how loud the cheers were when the announcer indicated each of us.

The humorous end to this story is probably what you already expect. First place was the karaoke singer who was built like an aging linebacker. Second place went to my new friend, Dallas. Personally, I thought she should have made number one. I was a bit jealous of her looks, lifestyle, and confidence if we're being totally honest. And third place friends? It was me. Surprise doesn't even begin to cover how I felt. Third place won me a child's sand pail full of swag which included a VHS copy of Bound, a T-shirt, hat, and a thirty-five-dollar credit at the bar. You want to know the best part of all? All three of us that won wore toe polish.

I'm older now and with my wife, who is amazing. We're good together and growing well into middle age rather than growing apart. Some folks aren't meant to be together. Some can't be better people until they're with someone who matches and inspires them. I wasn't that person with my ex and frankly I'm glad. I don't know how that person is now, or what their life is like. But I do know that I'm happy and different.

My journey has taken decades. I've spanned the gamut from looking like a twinkie gay boy, to a buzzed hair, softball, volleyball, football, and roller derby playing, butch. I came out as bisexual and came out again as gender fluid. When I was younger and in much better queer shape, I liked to throw folks off once in a while with a little black dress. I hate dresses, but it was a costume as much as anything I'd ever worn on Halloween. I don't like expectations or being put in a box. I still don't feel butch in attitude. I like to experiment with cooking, making soups and creating recipes. I still paint my toenails, wear eye liner on special occasions, and am obsessive about using nail files and hand lotion. But I also build cabinets, fix nearly all the stuff that gets broken, and I'm in charge of all the décor in the house because of my aesthetic sense. I have a technical job, I write books, am fascinated by puzzles, love math and reading, and excel at crushing people in yard games.

I still look pretty butch to most, being referred to as *sir* quite often. I'm less embarrassed by it now though. There is something that comes with age other than chronic knee pain, permanent weight gain, and the constant thought that *we were never that young at their age* in regard to our teenage sons. I think the person who saw the clearest version of me was a little old woman I met in 2014. My wife's grandma had seen me a few hours earlier at a surprise birthday party but we didn't meet until back at the house. My wife introduced us officially and that little old woman took my hands and said, "I thought you were her gentleman friend at the restaurant. Then you turned around and I saw your bosoms and feminine face. It's nice to meet you, dear." Then she tottered away to fill a red solo cup with wine from the fridge that she wasn't supposed to have or even know existed.

What I've learned in life is that butch is more than appearance, but your looks will set the expectation that you either pass or fail from. I've lived up and down to this expectation my entire life. Butch is nothing more than a costume, or aura that you put on to feel comfortable. It's armor to face a judgmental world for all those of us who don't fit in with that cis-straight society that expects you to be a feminine woman or masculine man, and certainly nothing in-between. It's attitude that you wish to project as part of your identity. Butch can be anything you want it to be as long as you have the courage and conviction to assert yourself.

My advice to anyone searching for their own identity who doesn't feel like they fit in is to break the boundaries, wreck the dynamic, and be fearless with your presentation. Accept *sir*, allow *ma'am*, but don't be afraid of your true self. There are many types of men in the world and so many ways to be masculine. The same can be said for women, agender, and transgender. If butch is part of your identity, then live it the way that feels best. Don't be afraid to celebrate the person inside that is you. That person is important.

Butch Is
By Giovanna Capone

vigorous female potency
a certain sensibility
a spirit as solid as a rock
She won't fit in anyone's box

Butch is female integrity
not masculinity.
It's mocking society's gender roles
living outside the box
trusting your ability to prevail
Butch is 100% female

Walking down the city streets
No mirror is there to reflect her
You gotta respect her individuality

She's a new kind of strong
a modern-day Amazon
It's been too long
since this woman
has gotten her due

You'd never guess
she's under duress
She covers it so well
you can hardly tell her pain

She may feign a calm serenity
but she'll never need your sympathy

Sometimes it's a battle to stay sane
especially after the pain
of a lover's rejection

She will cut her hair
wear her father's best shirts
and go on

Those around her
may despise her existence
But every day
she finds a way
to beat them back
and outlast them

It's an uphill climb
walking through a world full of land mines
With her thick soled leather boots
every day she lives, she wins

She's Brittney Griner
in a Russian prison camp
Six foot nine
leaves a permanent stamp
on your mind
She's one of a kind
and as she learned
it's a battle at every turn

One day she's in her power
The next day she prays for an hour
of peace

When she's at her worst
exhausted and sick

she feels the dearth of other women
who look like her
The scarcity is real
but she persists
tough as a Navy Seal
defying every social norm

Butch lesbians
are women in rare form
equal to the task
they are destined to outlast
every opposing force

They are modern day Amazons
walking through a hostile world
Butch women win the war
every day they prevail

Separations
By Giovanna Capone

Your next lover
will not gaze at a sweet young face
or stroke soft dark hair
No. You'll be older, weathered,
surer of what you want
and don't want.

Unfelled pine timber
your needle leaves
still green and intact in the cold
you are
ravenous and satisfied
at the same time,
a woman who knows
what strength she has
and uses it, building.

Your next lover
will have yellow brown skin
solid biceps
legs full of muscle, sinew, and nerve.
"Too political," "too intense,"
her entire being
is likely to seem
appalling at first.

Cut your brown hair
like you wanted it.
This time you

will be your next lover,
learned like one learns
the truths of the earth.

Moving endlessly through her seasons,
her changes happen
for no one,
begin unannounced,
and endure
as long as they need to.

To Have and To Be
By Susan Spilecki

I scan every crowd of women for you, thinking, Dapper butch seeks same for long-term monogamous snuggle-bunnies. If I could find you, you would be handsome and cuddly, with a square jaw and square shoulders. You would be a well-read woman with an impeccable vocabulary and you would grin and make me laugh. Those things are sexy as fuck. You would drag me off to the woods to camp and watch wildlife. You would sit home with me and watch superhero movies. We would sit with each other's pain, holding it gently in strong hands.

If I found you, it would be because they called us both sir and then apologized or threatened us and then backed down. It would be like looking in a rippling lake. You would not be my reflection, but the recognition on both sides would be instant. I have not met you yet. I have been trying to be you for half my life. If I found you, it would be like coasting downhill on a bike on a summer day, effortlessly coming home to your heat and the warm breeze of your breath in my ear.

If I find you and stammer my name, the women in skirts will stumble on their way to us, finally seeing that we are not there for them. The ones who decry labels will call us old-fashioned. The ones who embrace them will call us faggots. We will not hear a word above the rush and the percussion of our hearts. I have always been cautious when approaching a blind curve like self-presentation or love. If I find you, I will run, leap, crash into your strong waiting arms, kiss you with abandon, admire your boots.

When you find me as we shop for men's shoes in small sizes, we will laugh about sharing a wardrobe. When we cook together, you will impress me with your knife skills. You will teach me to play pool. I will teach you to tie a bowtie. We will teach each other to not run away from someone who offers a soft landing, not fear being too ready to help or build or teach the baby butches how it's done. We will not fear darkness. Prince Charmings, we will save each other in our dreams.

When we find each other, it will finally be easy. We will speak the same language, not just *high fade* and *Swiss Army*, but *sweetness* and *shared solitude*, *being needed* and *getting shit done*. We will forgive each other for hiding beneath our busy lives for so long. Maybe a late start isn't bad. The decades have made us experts. We have learned from all the mistakes. Giving too much, being too hard, refusing to feel, expecting to pay and pay. This time, we will finally do it right. This time, butch love will overcome.

And whether we take turns or go Dutch, sweet and swaggering, we will share our strength. Your hands on my skin will be hot. Your shudders in the dark dawn will last me all day, knowing I can make a wall crumble and build it back up again. We will harmonize my tenor with your alto. Even our hard conversations will become songs. We will laugh at ourselves while we share our burning passions. We will cry together when our stoicism fails. Your snoring will lull me back to sleep.

Together, we will take risks, take each other out to dinner in suits, tackle the Sunday crossword with a pen, challenge each other to be resilient rather than tough. Together, we will be safe. When you shoot your cuffs to show your cufflinks, I will swoon. When I write you sonnets, you will blush. We will be gentle with each other's hearts. Our eyes will be a hand-stitched quilt of chambray, denim, and pinstripe on one side, camo and Carhartt on the other. We will share neckties and cut each other's hair.

Let us indeed be butch for butch, not tearing each other down or hacking chinks from each other's armor. Some days, we will be warrior women and fight back-to-back. Other days, we will be boys climbing trees and sharing secrets. And even on days when we are girls, we will always, *always* be gentlemen, offering the world an arm to help them rise, a kind word to encourage, our muscles and sheer stubbornness to protect. Let us be brothers to each other, and sisters, lovers and friends. Some relationships are gold, some frankincense, and some glitter. So let us be fabulous.

Let us be effortlessly stylish like my cat and unbreakably loyal like your dog. Let us understand how, too often, institutions harm us and how, sometimes, knowing that you look good gives you courage to face and change the world. The right shoes, the right hair, the right attitude. The right human to hug and keep hugging, to sleep, spoon and dream with. To cook for, feed, and nourish. To offer flowers and a kind word. To spar with and grow strong. To love.

In a world where our family and friends are *either/or* and *neither/nor*, let us be *both/and*: a little yin, a little yang, a lot of heart. We balance each other. Your power tools and my poetry, your skin care regime and my kung fu, your brother's leather jacket and my father's vests. Let us every day be the best of both worlds, kind almost-women and conspicuous almost-men, tough and touchable, handy and soft-hearted. Friends and family will stand slack-jawed, but our plum boutonnieres will match.

On Being a Disabled, Butch Historian or: Not Walking With Two Ghosts
By Steph Ban

In my junior year of high school, the history teacher paused in his lecture on social relations in the 1950s.

"So all you boys would have been the breadwinners," he began. "And all you girls, what do you think you would have been?"

Some of the girls murmured to themselves, coming to his expected conclusion of housewife. I knew I wouldn't have been a housewife though, and not just because my full body recoiled at even the thought of wearing makeup or a dress. I don't remember if I raised my hand or not as I said "Institutionalized."

The resounding dead silence solidified three things— that I didn't fit in with others in my class, that I didn't have a place in the history my teacher wanted to tell, and that no one in the room knew what to do with those things.

This is an essay about how I study history. It's also an essay about being disabled, and an essay about being butch. I can't separate those three things, so I'm not going to. I had always known I wanted to study history, but that day in class added a new sense of urgency. I didn't want to be alone. I couldn't possibly be the only one experiencing what I did or feeling a crushing sense of isolation, even if I was the only wheelchair user in most rooms. Even if I liked a girl but was convinced she couldn't possibly like me back. Even if I didn't fit in with most other girls or boys my age and was half-convinced I must be an alien. I didn't even fit in with the other disabled kids in my physical therapy group, most of whom were significantly older or younger than me, and into either sports or playing dress up. I was also the only one who used a wheelchair full time. If I couldn't find others to identify with in the present, I would look to the past.

To college I eagerly went, determined to remedy my loneliness. College gave me many gifts, among them the feeling of having nothing to lose. Just before going away, I decided to tell the girl I liked that I liked her, and to my delighted shock, she felt the same way. This was the first counterpoint to my loneliness, and thankfully not the last. Finding disabled and queer communities, and the sizable overlap between them, was likewise a gift. I learned that disability was not something to be ashamed of, but something that could link me to others, past and present. I learned how to tap the table with the right pressure to get a deaf friend's attention, how to let a cane-using friend lean on my chair as I escorted her slowly across the quad, that the sense of relief I felt around many autistic people was really one of many signs I was one of them. I made trans friends for the first time. I learned about the nuances of sexuality, gender identity and expression, how it was okay to explore your identity and not to have everything figured out. I could talk about my relationship with my girlfriend openly and without fear. I cut my hair from mid-back-length to a pixie cut at age nineteen, right around the time I discovered what activist history was.

I was introduced to John Boswell's work for the first time in an introductory gender and sexuality studies class. The professor explained that Boswell was a gay historian drawing in part from his own lived experience to point out what he felt mainstream, heterosexual historians had overlooked— evidence of same-sex erotic love in premodern Europe. While my professor guided the class to think more about the ethics of applying the label of homosexual to people who did not have such a concept in their time, I felt like I had both fallen in love and found my purpose. History and identity didn't have to be separate. I hung back after class, and while I don't remember the entirety of what I said, which was probably a garbled mess.

I do remember telling her, *I want to do what Boswell does. I want to do that kind of history.*

Throughout college, I incorporated the frameworks of other activist scholars into my work, and in moments of doubt, whether self or externally imposed, each name became a bulwark, a concrete reminder that I wasn't alone in attempting to bridge my identity and my scholarship. Rosemarie Garland-Thomson, bell hooks, Sara Ahmed, Eli Clare, Audre Lorde. My presentation slowly drifted more masculine, supported mainly by flannels and opting not to remove my facial hair most of the time, and the first time I was called sir, bundled up in a coat and gloves in line at the café. I was surprised but not angry. It wasn't correct, exactly, but it didn't feel bad. I didn't know of their work at the time, but comedian Hannah Gadsby summed my feelings up well with their response to being called sir.

"Look, I don't identify as transgender, but I'm partial to a holiday." (Hannah Gadsby, *Nanette*)

Being mistaken for a man happens infrequently, usually in passing or by a young child still learning how to identify people, and it tends to upset others more than it upsets me. I know that I will always be read as disabled before I am read as having any particular gender. People tend to see my short hair and androgynous clothing as low maintenance for a disabled person rather than a conscious choice I make about my gender expression. There is definitely an element of practicality in my style, and rather than try to draw strict boundaries between what I do for disability reasons or gender expression reasons, I shrug and go about my day.

I thought I would go to grad school, study U.S. disability history, write a slightly edgy but ultimately respectable dissertation, and go on to a career as a slightly edgy but ultimately respectable professor. Then I read Jean-Jacques Rousseau's *Confessions*. I didn't even mean to read it. I was supposed to be reading about his educational philosophy. What started as skimming quickly became one of the most immersive experiences of my life, as I read Rousseau describe situations and feelings that felt ripped from my mind. Not knowing what to say when pressured to speak, intense, almost violent emotions that are impossible to describe when in their throes, feeling confined and out of place among new people and crowds, a burning wish that everyone simply communicated what they meant without layers of subtext, a sense that any language, spoken or written, could not contain the volume of my thoughts, and turning to solitude not only as preference, but as refuge when overwhelmed. I read *Confessions* during the course of roughly seven hours in one sitting. I paused only reluctantly at my girlfriend's urging to eat, and when the shaking that accompanies strong emotion or the blur of tears prevented me from seeing the computer screen. For the first time in my nearly four years of studying history and my nearly twenty-two years of life to that point, I had found someone who seemed to understand me instantly. I knew then that I could not exist in a world where I was not in some way in conversation with Rousseau, who seemed to experience disability in similar ways to me but without language for it.

As I delved deeper into why I, an obviously disabled, masculine of center queer woman in the twenty-first century U.S., felt so drawn to a racist, misogynistic, queerphobic Swiss philosopher of the eighteenth century who would undoubtedly hate me on sight, or at least view me with contempt, I learned something else. He too existed at the nexus of non-normative gender expression and disability. The long robe he wore in later life was in part a nod to his desire, perhaps jokingly expressed, but perhaps meant seriously, to "turn [himself] into a woman" (Leopold Damrosch, *Jean-Jacques Rousseau Restless Genius*), but also done to make his catheter use more discreet and easier to manage. (Jean-Jacques Rousseau, The Confessions of Jean-Jacques Rousseau, trans. J. M. Cohen) If the two of us could talk about gender as read through the context of disability, provided we could come to a shared understanding of either of those terms, I wonder what he'd say.

Luckily, Rousseau and I are not the only ones to navigate the spaces between disability and gender. Nonbinary writer Markie Burnhope notes that the disabled body is considered universally wrong in an ableist society that devalues disabled people regardless of their identification or disidentification with gender. (Markie Burnhope, "The Universal ' Wrong Body': My Own Non-Binary Trans Narrative," Vada Magazine) Burnhope details the convergence of degendering and infantilization through their experience of being addressed with terms leveled at children—buddy, pal, boss—rather than being viewed as an adult. Although they do not wish to be seen as a man, they experience being seen as a boy as disrespectful and jarring. (Ibid) As for myself, although I am a woman, I will gladly take *sir* over either *sweetie* or *buddy*. S.M. Neumeier likewise notes that "[d]isability is seen and treated as simultaneously emasculating and defeminizing." S. M. Neumeier, "Disabled Genders," Silence Breaking Sound (WordPress.com, June 19, 2015) I am inclined to agree. I'm not sure I'll ever be read as butch by the general public, so if my options are failing at femininity and being uncomfortable to boot, or being insufficiently masculine but comfortable in my skin, I choose comfort.

I'll tell you a few secrets, make a few confessions, as it were. One, I'm not stoic, which you probably figured out right around my description of sobbing profusely over a dead guy. Two, I'm afraid that by writing about Rousseau in this context, in this way, I will destroy any remaining chance I have to write about him as a subject of scholarly study. I'm not sure how many historians actually believe in objectivity, but by laying my cards on the table so completely here, I am declaring not only that I don't believe in objectivity, but that I am unwilling to act as if I believe in it, and proudly so. Three, although I have been describing myself as butch for several years now, I primarily used it as an aesthetic descriptor because I didn't know the history, which made me a bad historian. One of the reasons I didn't know the history is that I was afraid to face it, which made me a bad butch. The butches of the past were tough. They physically defended their communities. If they were disabled, they came by disability honestly, through struggle or as the result of violence, rather than by being born, like I did. I worry that if I'm not truly butch, then I am alone.

Recently, fed up with my own cowardice, I've been reading butch history and literature, reasoning that if I want to claim the label, I should have a clearer idea of what I'm claiming. I still have a long way to go and a long reading list. As expected, I found much that was admirable and made me appreciate what those before me endured so that I and others can exist. Also as expected, I found a lot that didn't quite fit me. I'm not physically strong enough to get out of bed without assistance, much less do physical labor. I didn't grow up playing outside with boys. I'm not going to be helping anyone move, unless they wish to hold my chair like a jet ski. I find no enjoyment in sports, and the answer to the hypothetical, *where would I be in the 1960s lesbian bar scene?* is still *institutionalized.*

What I didn't expect, however, was how much of what I read *did* resonate. When S. Bear Bergman writes about being, "a butch who relishes touch," (S. Bear Bergman, *Butch Is a Noun*) I remember that gentle headbutts and bear hugs that are abnormally strong coming from a woman are how I show love. When Jess in *Stone Butch Blues* pores over a few words in a historical record for just a glimpse at a life like hers, I recognize that feeling with my gut first, and I mourn the separations of time and space with her. I approached reading about proto-butch gentlewoman, Anne Lister, with curiosity, but I felt something click into place once I realized she also had read Rousseau and was moved by him. According to historian Anna Clark, Lister "...had to read Rousseau against the grain, emulating the way he used sexual frankness and androgyny to create a unique notion of the self, but rejecting his rigid attitudes toward women and homosexuality." (Anna Clark. "Anne Lister's Construction of Lesbian Identity." *Journal of the History of Sexuality* 7)

A few months ago, I saw Hannah Gadsby live. It felt wonderful to witness a fat, disabled, autistic butch being laughed with instead of laughed at. Before the show, I made tentative plans to meet up with a friend who I had thus far never met in person. Worried that I might not recognize them, I instructed them to approach me and my girlfriend.

I'll be the brunette butch in a power wheelchair, I messaged them.

It's a Hannah Gadsby show, they replied. *You may not be the only one.*

Clearly I Am Butch
By Zeeb

Clearly, I am butch
  I owned a truck for years
  I have hair just this side of a buzz cut
  My voice is low
  My body solid
  I walk with long strides
    and a confident air
  I walk like a dyke

My friend Rachel
  her frame thin and delicate,
  clothes flowing and long hair trailing
Can take down a 250-pound man
  with her black belt in Tae Kwan Do.

I have an impressive set of power tools
which I know how to use
I have built decks
  and roofed buildings
  and mounted drywall
  with the best of them
Yet my friend Tomoko
  painted nails and lipstick immaculate
  built out her van for camping
with the tightest fit and finish you've ever seen
While her lover, so clearly butch,
  sat inside and graded papers.

I fumble with my toaster oven
barely know how to operate my washing machine
nervously avoid the stove
while my friend Lupita
  ten times more butch than me
  pores over recipes

and sings in the kitchen.

I have more jeans than I can count
T-shirts enough for a decade
All my shirts are tailored
And I only wear V-neck sweaters (and down vests)
    yet my fingers trail over soft velvet
    and my closet harbors secret Hawaiian fabric
    My Birks have narrow straps
        (but they *are* Birks nonetheless!)

I keep my public face stone-y
My body poised for trouble
I hold my cards close to my well-covered chest
    Yet I let my lover touch me
    and moan softly when she does
I can be stopped breathless at the line of a poem
awestruck by a painting
cry watching a father playing with his toddler

I have tons of backpacks
and hiking boots
and camping equipment
Everyone who meets me pegs me as butch.
Clearly, I *am* butch.
Cleary, I am butch.

Whatever that means…

Why Did It Take So Long
By Susa Silvermarie

I'm a butch femme, though only now, in my prime of seventy-five years, do I realize that's what I have always been. A femme on the inside who's butch on the outside, that's me. It's not the same as a lesbian who is both butch and femme, though in younger decades I used to think I was both, maybe related to my Gemini birth chart, or to my having developed terrific flexibility during the course of partnerships with both butch lesbians and femme lesbians. But now I understand myself, my core natural self, as a butch femme.

As a butch femme I feel most comfortable in shirts and jeans, or, now that I live in Mexico, shirts and shorts and sturdy sandals. As a butch femme on a date, I go for a top that's simple and soft and sexy, over tight pants, maybe with a set of three earrings that look good together but are not a pair as such. A bright red sombrero to top it off here in Mexico. Maybe a scarf at the neck ala Oscar Wilde. A soft butch exterior but oh, melted butter inside. Do you know the old expressions, butch on the street, femme in the sheets? A true femme who looks butch, like me.

And as a butch *femme*, I will likely never stop watching for the butch of my dreams. How will I know her? She will feel protective of me, the way I have always felt protective of my lovers. She will initiate erotic play at the drop of a sombrero, and be tender in a most ferocious manner, that is, a manner deliberate and slow, listening attentively for my nuanced responses. She will explore me like a new galaxy and open me to the widest multiverse ride. My femme core will trust this butch of my dreams with everything I am, though I will not be a whit concerned with what her outward style appears to be.

I have been so rich in love. My gratitude goes out into my past for every woman who has ever loved me into being. My wealth of loving relationships has honed my sensibilities and my soul.

Though I speak from more than fifty years of

experience as a lesbian, it is my herstories as an elder lesbian that have been the deepest. How could it be otherwise? We have so much more to bring to one another as we evolve into age, so much more self-knowledge and spiritual development and tested paths. However, looking back through the curtain of time at myself in the seventies and beyond, I can clearly see flashes of the butchy femme I didn't know I was.

There was that evening in Cambridgeport with Ellen, when we were making out in the woods near the murmuring of the Charles River. A public park, yes, but usually empty, and in those days no streetlamps to disturb the velvet darkness of the night. I hardly realized Ellen and I had ardently stripped one another, and every article of our clothing was strewn about the base of the tree against which we leaned together in ecstasy. The sudden sound of approaching footsteps made us freeze. A man came into full view. I leaped to my feet and ran the few steps to face him. Not even thinking about my nakedness, I anchored my karate stance directly in front of him, primed to kick or punch. My eyes wild with power, I distinctly remember the fear in his. Doesn't sound very femme, does it. You'd be surprised. I experienced it as a spontaneous butch move by a fiercely protective femme Mama.

Here's another vignette that unfolded with a much softer feel. It was waltz night at the Orange Peel, and my honey whirled me around the dance floor all evening long. She didn't swagger, and she wouldn't have called herself a butch for the world, but she was a big bright sensuous woman, and she wanted to please me. It was my dream come true. I was so ecstatic I couldn't stop grinning. Right there at the *Orange Peel Social Aid and Pleasure Club*, I tilted my head back in utter surrender, in the most authentic femme swoon I have ever known. It doesn't sound butch, does it? You'd be surprised. You can't always peg a butch or a femme, or a butch femme, or a femme butch.

One more example of the lovely slippery spectrum. Not so long ago at all, I was on a date, all giddy with new love. After a romantic dinner out, she drove us down to the lakeshore. The moon was dancing a path full on the water, and it felt like happiness was walking with us. We kissed in public that night, sitting on a bench, not caring about the few folks passing by. When a breeze came up and I rubbed my arms, she took off her jeans jacket and tenderly draped it over my shoulders. I don't think she knew I adored her jacket from India with all its colorful embroidery, a garment tough enough to be butch and soft enough to be femme. I can still feel her placing it on me. Later when we were saying goodnight, and I started to take it off, she told me to keep it. I looked in her eyes and ran my hands down the arms, as if I were smoothing them down hers. When I wear the jacket even now, I often find myself performing that gesture.

Why did it take so many decades to understand myself as a femme on the inside who's butch on the outside? Back in the seventies, almost all of us new lesbian-feminists adopted a butch look when we came out, partly simply to recognize one another, partly to demonstrate rejection of hetero mores for women. Most of us newbies had zero understanding of the depths of traditional butch and femme identity, or of the survival herstories from which such identity emerged. I am ashamed to admit we thought we were better than the old butches and femmes who sometimes still came to the bars we were taking over. In our ignorance, we disparaged them as engaging in mere role-playing or imitation.

Femme was especially confusing to us in those days, before the brilliant work of Joan Nestle and others, who differentiated it from its superficial hetero version. But the first time I heard, butch on the street, femme in the sheets, some part of me knew it was more than description. It was an internal identity that fit. Now at last I can own with pride this style that is natural for me, this orientation of my orientation. I'm a butch on the outside, who, on the inside, is as femme as they come!

From Dad's Shirt to a 15-Foot Closet
By John Dominic

Being butch, to me, means feeling my most authentic and empowered self, being totally a woman who is deeply drawn emotionally to women and is sexually attracted to other women – some femme, some butch and some who don't identify as either.

Attire is one of my most significant gender expressions. For me, like some others, cross dressing would be wearing clothing from the women's department. I wear clothes typically found in the men's department. But as Leslie Feinberg said of the suit she was wearing at one of her presentations at the Women's Building in San Francisco— "If I bought it and I'm wearing it, is this a man's suit?"

I identify my style for both dress and casual wear as that of a banker, i.e., traditional, classic, tailored style and fit with much Virgoan attention to detail. This is accompanied by an innate passion for vintage formal wear, a possible bleed-through from another life. It ranges from top hat, white tie and tails to a 1930s double breasted hourglass tuxedo, to a morning suit with its gray stripe trousers, wing tip collar shirt, peak lapel vest, ascot with stick pin, charcoal cutaway coat, complete with a pearl-gray top hat and matching gloves. I am also partial to period dress costumes.

Along with mannerisms, gestures, sexuality, spirituality, stance, energy and vulnerability, this external sartorial gender expression falls under Judy Grahn's observation in her book, *Another Mother Tongue,* (Judy Grahn, *Another Mother Tongue Gay Words Gay Worlds*) that butch is "…a useful description of another way of being female…" (p.61). Constrained by our limited patriarchal language, butch is my core identifier. In an Amazon Nation, there would be a plethora of descriptors.

My pronouns are she/her. I love and like my female woman's body including and especially my breasts. I find it very erotic to come home from a wonderful social evening of dancing, dining, partying, symphony or theatre with my honey and get undressed or be undressed by her – from untying the bow tie to uncovering my breasts under the lavender lace bra or a white T-shirt. Then getting into bed as the two beautiful women we are, each totally inhabiting her female body as an offering to the other. My psyche, brain and body are female and different from a male person, who wants to have a male body to match his psyche and brain.

In *The Persistent Desire,* Joan Nestle writes of Deanna Alida— "She was buried in her tuxedo.… Her butch self was not a masquerade or a gender cliché, but her final and fullest expression of herself." (p.20). When I am dressed in my truth, I feel fully empowered. This authentic gender expression through clothing emboldens me to take new risks, to communicate from my heart, to not be as guarded. Thespian Michael Wayne Turner III, whose wardrobe is completely vintage, said in the *San Francisco Chronicle Datebook* May 14, 2022, that following his designated sartorial guidelines, he feels like a superhero. My nomenclature of choice for myself is dyke dandy. Turner also states: "Black dandyism is an attitude, an identity and a way to be free." He continues, "The attitude of the dandy is this complete acceptance and recognition of a complex mind expressed in clothing." Though coming from different historic and cultural contexts, I share these sentiments and that dandyism is whimsical, playful and yet serious, intellectual, cultured, sophisticated.

I experience my truest reality and am more easily present only when dressed in the clothes that connect me to my real self. For me, the ritual of putting on these clothes is spiritual and an evocation of my gender spirit. I feel relaxed and confident wearing vintage or later formals, but I'll acquiesce to a suit and tie if the occasion doesn't afford formal wear.

This particular fashion affinity seems to have always been integral to me. As a septuagenarian butch, seared in my mind are recollections of—

At age three, being aware of the rich emotional feel of my Dad's white cotton business shirt.

At age four, appreciating how the boy's red corduroy western pants, vest and shirt set, a birthday present from my uncle, was like my Dad's clothes. The shirt had a collar and cuffs and the pants' zipper was in the front – a bonanza for this baby butch.

Thinking, both times my mother was pregnant, that if the baby was a boy, I could choose his clothes and dress him the way *I* wanted to dress. Both were girls.

Visiting my great Aunt Lizzie in the nursing home, where some residents made handcrafted articles displayed for sale in the hall curio cabinet. I chose the hand-span high groom doll dressed in a morning suit and removable shiny black plastic top hat that I could take off and put back on.

Asking my seamstress Grandmother to make a suit for my little boy doll, John. I instructed her to add side stripes down the trouser legs, which she did with thin strips of matching satin ribbon.

Choosing a unisex snowsuit during the 1950s, more than a decade before this fashion was popularly called unisex. I loved wearing this outfit, even when it prompted a neighborhood kid to ask if I was a girl or a boy, which disquieted me.

Each night, as a little girl, putting on my matching pajama bottoms and long-sleeved, collared top, left untucked, pretending it was a suit, then combing my daytime bangs to the side.

Wishing I could have the out-grown clothes of our neighbor's son, whose parents were going to donate them to charity. I said nothing because I knew I wasn't supposed to seriously want to wear clothes that were not girls clothes.

Watching closely how the salesman at our neighborhood haberdashery looped the long tie material around his finger to demonstrate to my mother how it would look tied in a four-in-hand slipknot when worn. To this day, I use the technique.

Figuring out that for my Girl Scout troop's Halloween party I could wear my late grandfather's tuxedo if I went as a magician. To complement the look, I found a St. Patrick's Day cardboard top hat in the cellar, painted it black and stuffed it with paper towels so it would stay on my head. Wearing these clothes, I felt ecstatic the whole night.

Sporting Dad's cuff links on my high school uniform shirt cuffs with great pride. The uniform also had a weskit and a simple variation of a bow tie. Unfortunately, skirts were de rigueur.

Encouraging my dad, throughout the seventeen years I lived at home, to wear cuff links, bow ties and his fedora but he was not one to wear a hat save for the rare blizzard. His injured fingers on one hand made it too difficult to secure cuff links and bow ties.

Sartorial recollections of my adult life are of passionately developing and evolving my wardrobe and wearing these frocks on every possible occasion, with a penchant for raising the level of dress a notch up from what was called for. The wardrobe increased incrementally until a fifteen-foot long, double rod, double shelf closet was replete with vintage and other finds from thrift stores to off the rack retail to orders filled at The Custom Shop, a purveyor of properly fitting shirt collars since 1937. My very first visit was at the New York store in 1968.

Every morning, putting on a newly laundered and pressed shirt with a suit or with trousers and a blazer was an exhilarating ritual to begin each workday. Assembling a day's finery with the appropriate accessories nourished my aesthetic sensibilities and enlivened my gender spirit. Overall, accessories included any variety and combination from my collections of gloves, hats, vests, cuff links and shirt front stud sets, pocket handkerchiefs, suspenders, belts, shoes, ascots, four-in-hand, long ties and bow ties.

As much as I would have gloried in wearing a tie to work, as an elementary school teacher and administrator, I didn't have the courage. I wasn't fooling anyone who saw this butch—short hair, no lipstick or earrings, no purse —no saving factor. This was a lurking piece of my own internalized homophobia. Then came the weekends, a dance outfit including a tie for every Friday night and whatever the weekend socials elicited.

In my early days of creating suitable sartorial choices for myself, I went to a jobber's outlet in Los Angeles to find something that would feel good to wear to a co-worker's wedding. There it was, a striking outfit of black dress pants with a white vest and jacket to which I added a deep pink satin shirt. The salesman was very solicitous until the purchase was paid for, at which point he became curt and discourteous. However, I felt good in it at the wedding and every time I wore it.

In the mid-1970s, a male member of the Imperial Court of San Jose invited me to escort her down the runway at their annual ball. This was my very first time renting a formal – all white tails and top hat. After that, renting continued until I found the Selix Formal Wear used department. Thus, began the adventure of owning a varied formal wardrobe.

The Captain's Dinner on board the first attempted all lesbian cruise, which sailed to Bermuda in 1987, called for a tuxedo. Before Olivia Records expanded to running cruises, this one was organized by women entrepreneurs out of Pennsylvania. Their effort realized one hundred twenty-five lesbians out of the six hundred passengers who sailed. The lesbians identified certain areas on the ship to congregate. While everyone had access, the lesbians either dominated or took over these spots. In the casino, after the Captain's Dinner, we wound up in mixed company, i.e., lesbians and straights. One of the straight women asked if my partner and I would agree to have our picture taken. She came across as respectful and we said yes.

For Halloween, I would start contemplating months ahead – choosing, planning and securing my character and costume. Who would be released this year? These are some of the characters who lived vicariously through me for a Halloween night.

Johnny Town-Mouse, Beatrix Potter's impeccably dressed, early 1900s urban rodent.

West Point Cadet in parade uniform with its stiff, high-crowned, peaked black hat accented by the plume.

Scottish Highlander from the movie, *The Barkley's of Broadway* from1949, a character from the show within the show, outfitted in a kilt and regalia.

Fashionable mid 1750s English Gentleperson, dressed to the nines, wearing a full skirted floral pastel print coat with large front pockets and deep sleeve cuffs with extended inches of ruffled lace on the shirt sleeves, a long wine-colored vest with large metal buttons, a multi-lace layered jabot front, a feathered three-cornered hat and buckled shoes.

Femme partner – Having had exchanged clothes and hair styles, as we entered the dance floor, the other regular dance attendees, thinking they knew who they were seeing, did double takes to decipher the scene – a great success.

Summer formal – I used the occasion of Halloween on the Castro in San Francisco to dress in formal wear, black satin striped trousers, bow tie, cummerbund, cuff links and shirt studs with a white, shawl lapel, single breasted dinner jacket and linen pocket handkerchief. My companion dressed, head to toe, as a vibrator complete with an operating power switch.

United States Marine with my femme pal, both of us were in full dress uniforms including hats and white snap gloves.

John Radclyffe Hall was my response to a lesbian couple's Halloween wedding invitation to attend dressed as a lesbian of your choice. I wore a midnight blue blazer and homburg hat set off by a white dress shirt and midnight blue bow tie with classic small white dots as per her photograph.

Easter is another dress up holiday. I rented my first morning suit for an Easter Sunday. Having experienced the thrill and transformation of wearing it, when I returned it on Monday, I promptly ordered one of my own. I could delight in wearing it at will for any possible occasion or make up my own, as I have for the past three decades. Thus, began an annual custom of Easter brunch and a stroll along the Castro with adorned friends.

One particular year, I participated in the Easter Bonnet Contest at MCC in San Francisco. Many gay men would spend the day before Easter at the local florist on Castro Street visualizing and crafting their bonnets for the next day's multiple categories of competition. I entered the contest in the spirit and tradition of the Easter Parade down Fifth Avenue as immortalized by Fred Astaire and Judy Garland in the movie of the same title, set in 1912. My morning suit with its pearl-gray top hat and contrasting black grosgrain band would actually be appropriate. This, most assuredly, was *my* best bonnet and in one category—I don't remember which one— I received first place. I was happy for the recognition and validation.

Appropriately, it was in a theatre that a fantasy turned real. While being one of the stage crew, but this night dressed in full tails, I waltzed backstage with my cast member partner along with other formally clad cast members of "The Merry Widow" to the live orchestral music as the actors played the scene on stage.

The Art Deco Society of California (ADSC) has always encouraged Deco period dress for its members and guests for all its occasions. Its grandest events are the annual themed Preservation Ball in the spring and the Gatsby Picnic on the lawn of the Dunsmuir Historic Estate, Oakland, CA, in the fall. This outdoor transfiguration was when period everything came into play. The goal was authenticity in every aspect. Simple to sumptuous picnic spreads arrived in wicker or rattan baskets carrying china plates, cloth napkins and wax paper wrapped savory goodies packed in tin boxes. No plastics or electronics, though a few were kept out of sight. Classic automobiles transported guests from the property entrance to the picnic site and then they were all parked on display for picnic goers to admire and appreciate up close. Parasols, dropped waists, boater hats, newsboy caps and plus-four sport knickers were all the rage. During the years, among the popular fashion choices of the Deco period, I chose double breasted vests, white flannel or light-colored trousers with button-type suspenders, solid or striped blazers with brass buttons, plus-four knickers with argyle or decorated high socks, two tone spectator shoes, a cap or boater hat, shirts in solids or stripes with white collar and cuffs and bow ties. Both a hat and tie were necessary to meet the proper social conventions of the day. A live orchestra played Deco era dance music throughout the afternoon incorporating Charleston and foxtrot tunes and highlighting the Deco Belles Dance Troupe. Interspersed in the activities were contests for dancers, picnic setups, costumes and beautiful babies. Guided tours of the mansion and games, such as croquet, rounded off the day.

Any visit to London required stopping for the feeling of home at Saville Row to visit the historic bespoke suit shops as well as Jermyn Street businesses for their custom shirts. Several of these establishments have signed registers on display going back hundreds of years. The continued quintessential quality of their fabrics and fine work is textile orgasm to the touch.

To elicit as much dress up as our guests would enjoy, the invitations to our marriage ceremony read Daytime Formal at the bottom. At the celebration, we were flanked by the wedding party, which was comprised of the best butch, the bride's butch co-mother, a dozen handsome butch friends all bedecked in morning suits and boutonnieres and twelve beautiful femme friends who stepped out in their choice of dresses and glorious chapeaux, several in grand picture frame style.

A time-honored practice and occasion for dress were the

birthday luncheons, three times a year with friends at Scott's Seafood Restaurant, always a window table on the water in Jack London Square, Oakland.

A Christmas Eve custom with a group of friends was attending the Gay Men's Chorus of San Francisco Christmas Concert at the Castro Theatre along with the shared merriment of a holiday dinner at a gay restaurant. This was an annual opportunity to be warm in my full Inverness cape and top hat worn over a black velvet dinner jacket, crisp white wing tip collar shirt with small stone ruby cuff links and studs, a bow tie of ruby red satin and finished with a hand hemmed white linen pocket handkerchief.

Beyond the elation of donning period dress, being immersed in the era was a total experience. This was what Nevada City, CA created with the Victorian Christmas Faire. Staying at the legendary National Hotel added to the ambiance of being in the midst of Victorian times. At night, the main street was closed to cars and filled with bright decorations and gas lit lampposts. The steepled chapel, and all the historic buildings, were silhouetted in lights against the dark winter sky. Shops and restaurants were all open, cheerily decorated and warmly lit to welcome guests. One of the many Victorian street vendors roasted chestnuts on an open fire for all who wished to partake. Carolers and musicians, in period costumes, mufflers and hats, scarves and gloves, strolled the street sing-ing and playing joyous holiday melodies. Many of the towns-people dressed in period style and visitors were greatly encouraged to enjoy wearing Victorian garb. I joined the fes-tivities, well turned out, in white tie with tails, Inverness cape, Victorian top hat and black leather gloves. For, yet, one more authentic Victorian encounter, a horse drawn carriage was driven through the town and along the surrounding residential side streets for an evening ride back to the National Hotel.

Anne Lister (1792-1840), the Halifax, West Yorkshire lesbian landowner, came to popularity through Sally Wain-wright's writing and co-directing of the Gentleman Jack series. Always on the lookout for opportunities to dress up, another OLOC, or Old Lesbians Organizing for Change, affiliate and I were in the planning stages of presenting a readers' theatre pro-gram about Anne Lister to the Bay Area chapter. First, in the order of things, I had assembled all the parts of an Anne Lister costume to include a period black floor length opera coat, Victorian top hat, black ascot, horseshoe vest, leather gloves and a wooden walking stick. Alas, Covid caused all gatherings to cease and we never did decide on the selections from Lister's diary entries. If it ever resurfaces, the wardrobe is at the ready.

There were many other venues and occasions where and when I dressed up, some no longer functioning.

Standouts for me were BACW, the Bay Area Career Women monthly meetings and Puttin' on the Ritz annual Pride celebration formal ball, NCLR, National Center for Lesbian Rights, annual spring awards dinner and entertainment, Tilden Ball, Brazilian Room, Tilden Park, Oakland, annual, Butch Femme Socials of the San Francisco Bay Area, and Butch Femme Conferences, a four-day, nationwide event held in New Orleans, Las Vegas, et al.

Others were women's music concerts. The Patio restaurant on Castro Street Sunday brunch outdoors, Drag King Nights, Oakland, Berkeley Chamber of Commerce annual fete, and Ashram assemblies, Oakland. Also, of interest to me are movie showings inviting all to come in costume as a favorite character. At the *Sound of Music* I dressed as Captain Von Trapp. Most recently, Florence Douglass Center, Vallejo, CA sponsors monthly themed dinners with music, dancing and entertainment. Dress up is optional and fun for many. My personal favorite was the Gatsby theme.

For me, the *hardest* thing about being butch is using the women's room in public places. I don't.

The *best* thing about being butch is being happy. I wouldn't be happy living out any other identity.

Rapture
By Rowan Harvey

I'm not a religious woman. My mother raised me Christian, until she didn't, then tried to raise me Buddhist, until she stopped that, too. My father, a man married to logic and facts and *not* my mother, is an atheist to the core. I took a single theology course in my first semester of college and failed it.

I know, however, that Sundays are often considered holy. Days of rest, they're called. Many stores close early or don't open at all and regular church service is early in the morning.

Now, don't forget, I'm not a religious woman. Not particularly spiritual, either. Nonetheless, I pray. I worship. I hold deep faith. More than that, I love and devote myself unconditionally to my Goddess and the temple in our shared bathroom.

My faith is tied deeply to who I and the Goddess each are as beings. I am a small, grubby, rough little creature. I am soil, in my ways. Full of life, full of love, and ever-changing.

My Goddess, by both contrast and compliment, is a soft-haired, flower-scented star which shines so much kinder than the sun. Not blinding, not distant, rather she is a consistently soft force in my world.

She is the reason I recognize Sundays as holy. Each time the week ends, she calls to me sweetly, my benevolent siren, and I join her in the temple. I strip to nothing but my cheap boxers and wait for her to approach.

She takes her time ensuring the razor is clean of all previous uses. This time, much like the last and the next, is its own. No past evidence may linger.

Once the blades are clean, she guides me to sit on the edge of the bathtub. The temple is modest, without any seating or room for two people. Nonetheless, the Goddess makes it work.

I do not stare as she fits the eighth-inch guard in place. Instead, I close my eyes and await her touch.

She always starts gently. Her skin meets mine before she begins, soft hands cupping my face, running hands through my quarter-inch hair. Rather than melt, I sink. I drift quietly from the physical temple into a more nebulous place of worship, a place devoid of anything save for her presence.

Then, without any more preamble, I am tethered back to my godly reality by the humming of the razor. My eyes remain shut and she tilts my head back and forth, running the blades across my scalp with perfect method. My eyelids flutter as she clips. The pressure of the plastic guard on my head brings a grounding pain to my nerves.

I feel no qualms in letting myself sigh, enthralled by her touch. Otherwise, we are both silent. No chatter fills the air. It's necessary to the ritual that no words are shared.

Once she finishes, she brushes her hand across my scalp a single time. She catches fine hairs in the grooves of her palm, though it doesn't bother her. I leave my eyes shut. I am content. Happy in the purest sense. I don't want to break such a tense and beautiful atmosphere.

My eyes must open at some point, though, and when they do, my Goddess is wreathed in fluorescent light, staring at me with a yet-incomprehensible look. I stare back, meeting her eyes for the first time since she began. As she finishes her appraisal, she asks me how it feels. I touch my shorn hair and speak one word, perfect.

She doesn't smile. Instead, she leans down to my level and her eyes drift closed, mirroring mine. We both know what ends the ritual.

The kiss is delicate. It is a prayer, a promise, and a deep gratitude wrapped in one perfect touch.

I am not a religious woman. I don't believe that a deity lives inside or above us. Rather, I know that the only goddess that exists lives on Earth, in my apartment, with myself and our two dogs.

When I Met Haruka
By M.A. Dubbs

I met her at a workshop class,
in a former life
deep set eyes and thick blonde brows,
like a Midwest version of Mr. Wickham.
I know that he is fun
but no good
but I guess we all have a catch
and I'm eager to find out hers.
She captures my eyes with a short intensity
that feels like an hour.
She says we can call her whatever,
and she's so cool
as she rests her ankle on her knee,
hands laced behind her neck,
energy to take up the entire space
of this classroom.

A poet by hobby,
former soldier by trade,
she is about the pretty nurses
that treated her overseas.
I can't help but wish her a mild catastrophe
so I could be by the bedside
and help her mend.
Can't look up from editing
without a greeting from her wide,
white knowing smile,
so I'll play prairie dog between
my prose and her gaze instead.

When we meet at an open-mic,
she's dressed to the nines:
dark blue power suit
on a 5'5" frame

and a blonde slick back
that rests on her shoulder pads.
I tell her that she's so GQ.
She says she doesn't know what that means
but she likes the way I say it
so it must mean something good.
I get an offer of her sports coat
because it's a shame I look so cold
in a dress so nice.

When she's on stage, she fills the room
like she is nothing but Earth.
A real-life Haruka.
She loves fast cars
and pretty girls
and I wonder if she wants a blond, bi
Michiru of her very own?
She's one of the few eyes I can see
when I go up to read,
as she nods her head to tell me
it works.

At semester's end,
she tells me I write about the dark
and ugly things of this world.
As parting words,
I tell her I just can't write about beautiful things.
Perhaps you'll read this, Haruka,
and tell me that I'm wrong?

Possibility
By Claudia R. Asch

To live, not dream what's possible now
To bend the binary
To exist in this body
Mostly without fear
Surprisingly unnoticed at times

Except when there is the choice to make
To relieve myself
Man
Woman
Male
Female
Tick a box and then all will be well

Questions arise
Who and what now?
Are you allowed here, *am I in the right bathroom*
What's right or wrong about relief of bodily fluids
It is a human right

And even if I don't compute in your eyes
I'm unapologetically real
And will not make myself small again
To fit in the binary box

Post Pandemic Butch Dream
By Claudia R. Asch

When I put on a shirt
And a tie
I feel more alive
More bright
Tying that knot
Feels like setting the butch free—finally
The smart trousers
The belt
Sometimes a waistcoat
Sometimes a V Neck jumper
To ensure the tie pops
The brogues
The jacket
My second skin
My chosen armour
I perceive the looks
Fleeting, mostly
There's some admiration
Definitely confusion
Who, what is that…
They can think what they like
For the first time, I feel handsome, attractive
I feel authentic
I am in technicolour
Stood defiantly between the binary chairs
In my smart, sexy suit

Butchness—A Compass

By S.E. Smyth

For years and years, I've been butch, a long-haired butch, a tomboy, a soft-butch. Still, I never quite had the commanding yell in your ear, hard butch mystique. Years and years, I didn't know I was a lesbian. How could you not know? Common response.

In the rural woods, in small old industrial and factory towns, in rural communities, women don't always wear lipstick. It's common for wives with husbands to drive ATVs and also cook or hunt, eat jerky. Women don't always have the same place. Pink camo is deceptive, confusing for a vegan suburbanite.

So, when I went to a rural campus and then a job in a more rural national forest, where women leaders wore pants, changed tires, and also had husbands, I was confused. Did butchness amount to emotion and feeling or attitude and convenience? My internalized homophobia rambled. Maybe things would be just easier, for life, to move around as someone straight who also has these feelings. Maybe it would be easier to hide. All the while, my inner voice said you know better. You are gay.

But who knows a mountain woman's partner is really a beard, and who knows why that one butch woman is so much of a recluse? No one really discussed being gay around a certain type of man in a run-down rural town. I counted one rainbow pride flag in fifty square miles. I sought them every day, every car ride to a new place, and still I couldn't stop thinking about that first one I saw. I met a young trans kid who worked at the gas station just outside of town months and months later. Somehow. I got a coffee every day on my way to work. And life kept passing by.

Each butch has a unique set of circumstances. Mine differ just like the rest. A loose count of butch stories tallies that most knew they were queer early on. I didn't have that voice in the back of my head until the end of high school. At seven, my He-Man dress up costume, complete with belt, sword, and wrist cuffs, just didn't cue me in about my difference. Still, when I got lost in the woods with only my toy compass, I knew crying was for girls. I knew I didn't want to cry, and I knew that I did. I've come to realize that both these things are okay.

Butchness, however appearance-oriented the concept may be, attaches to emotion. A good deal of us may not see the linked emotion because of swagger, nonchalance, and stoic natures. Because they are so damn sexy. My life doesn't necessarily encapsulate what it is to be or feel butch. With or without late proclamations or early guesses, I filtered toward a standard butch appearance early on. Still, behind the barrier, the image I gravitate and gravitated toward, I sense similar feelings that appear. If I can tap with a pick at one emotion that butches take in and distribute, though the world doesn't always see it, it is friendship and bonding. The need to associate, to find comradery, finally relax, is paramount. Finding someone like you, a role model, is so affirming, yet so elusive in rural areas. That, with my wife, I feel.

****

The underwear section of the department store, for a butch woman, is a wild jungle fraught with danger and beasts. Entering this situation, just before the turn of the century, as a teenager, several things ran through my head. I'm wearing men's clothing, and the salesclerk doesn't like it. I'm just buying underwear for my girlfriend, so what. Jeez, lady, at least I'm not in the men's section. Mantra—No one cares. No one cares. No one cares.

The only thing I can say is women's underwear shopping required patience and humbleness. I didn't have a big butch, a guide, or a role model. I had myself, my identity, my difference, and confidence in that, not the word lesbian as much. You can do it. It is so easy because it is who you are and if it's boyish or butch from ground up, from days without dresses, arguments at five about having no clothes at all or tinkering with trucks instead of dolls. Blocks are for boys, my brother always said, and after that I went directly for them.

I didn't have someone to say, this is how you shop for underwear. I bought what I bought without pride. The clerks whispered behind a desk. The register, theft, ran through my head. It would be time eventually to wash my hand over my face, pull off the sweat, turn the dial to cold and pale, and pony up.

I knew as much to shop at ten in the morning on a Thursday. But a few shoppers lingered, peeked from behind racks with their own slightly questionable interests. They hovered to see, shuffled closer to the cashier, listened as I grabbed and stalked cold deliberate steps to escape as soon as possible. A paranoia surfaced that marijuana couldn't imitate. My life, my lack of dignity displayed for a few strangers to bat around, cat, ball.

Had someone instructed me how to insert a tampon, I would have had a much easier time in school. Blood overflowed. Others laughed. Experiments happened. Words went unspoken because my friends were boys. Girls may have talked amongst themselves. I will never know. A stranger with a problem and no one to go to, I suffered as others don't describe. No one told me about cramps. A godsend would've been a friend, of a similar butch character, that would accept questions, not to be respoken, strict confidence from also knowing the severity of distrust. Someone who knew the same. Someone who, in two words, would tell me what I needed to know and then drop it. They left me without.

****

I wasn't quite in a happy place when I started digging in the dirt, a very butch occupation. Years and years I knew I was gay, err, a lesbian. I justified the profession of archaeology mostly to avoid having to wear women's business clothes, often seen as overdressed for a twenty-year-old, or mind you, skirts. Years and years of education, philosophy at best, to avoid shopping for hours to find something work appropriate without creping, ruffles, or any of a variety of details that might indicate femininity. Years before non-binary clothing, locations where men's clothing might not go over, might I say, so well, and rainbows decorated common store logos for a month, I suffered.

It was archaeology, actually and figuratively. The word lesbian hadn't yet surfaced with confidence. Apart from the work, the community of dirt diggers, I existed. None of us, the young group, were yet okay with the place, the grime under our fingernails, the gas station breakfasts, the budget motels. Decades later, we would look back and say work was so difficult because cheap manual labor is so taxing.

The dry dirt smeared across my head as the sweat profusely came. I sweat more than most, more than those considered abnormal, so when the perspiration flowed as a stream, they all looked. The glances may or may not have been in regard to my queerness, my otherness, the pills I kept at home. I still did not quite fit in.

My greatest find? Some dirt and a few stones and some doll's eyes that could've slipped through the cracks of a well-worn, employee built, archaeological screen.

This group of young women, a man or two, were those I listened to, checked for clues. I wondered every hour, which one is the lesbian, which one is gay? And when I found a new job, when I left because of the burden of my thoughts, when that rural run-down place overwhelmed me too much, I knew none of them were gay. The rough clothing, flannels from the men's section, the muscles. Still, yet, they were not wrapping their arms around women at night. My intuition counterbalanced my hopes. This much I left or left them in their own lies.

This experiment in butchness as a profession let me know that there is aloneness, emptiness exists, and I knew I needed to fill the void with someone, a woman, a person still, as these young women were, like me. When I knew I was butch and I wanted to look through the mirror, I started my hunt for lesbians. And I took off, or more so, got accepted into a big city, and living was all kinds of terrifying. I saw and wanted, and felt again left behind, just a woman catapulted from a small town, not quite in, before she was even out.

****

Coming out in a small town is not without complication. Circa 2000, the nightmare doubled. In the next small town I got stuck in, sentiments resounded two-fold. When I finally escaped, moon-shot to a city, the shock of people knocked me off balance by itself. The attitudes and sneers, the inability to accept jeans and a sweatshirt as acceptable fashion debilitated me. I took to my indoor basement apartment, stayed there, read graduate school readings, basked a little, and marinated. I developed an awkward relationship with the virtual space Second Life. Friendship was difficult to come by. Buried, I was dead and gone. One fine lover would eventually resurrect me and tell me that I was, in fact, also a divine being, a lesbian. Later, in the right place.

I moved back to a small town. In that city, I had a vision and hope. I dreamed about moving back to a small town to be comfortable and secure in my surroundings, away from pretentiousness and attitude. My dream materialized into a town much like the one in my vision, with a woman much like the one who I love now. I am in this place and feel safe and myself. My butch second life, one with my lover. With the full span of my wings, I could fly anywhere. I stretch them often with her, but always end up back in this same town. The small house flies a rainbow pride flag. I didn't have to pray, but I imagined, and poof. With a new history to look back on, I can say that this is honestly my happy place, and I could never leave.

The first time I said the word lesbian, the gays released a flock of doves. Butch came out just after, even if I didn't introduce myself at work as butch, my-self knew. I carried the word, held it with me. After years of pent-up emotion, I'm here finally, signed on to be queer full time. Non-binary, a host of other terms. Anything but lesbian—sneers. I think back to how long it took me to say the word. My decade or so wrestle with the fact that I thought the word gay when I meant lesbian. Lesbian is such a syllabic word and takes so long to think. Was it not just easier to think and want to say you were gay… if you spoke it… if you ever said the words?

When I said the word so, so many years later, the proclamation was monumental. I articulated the sound cognizant of the way the noise felt in tandem with the motions of my mouth.

I was the embodiment. I expressed it. And the announcement took me oh, so long. It felt so good. And now they say, *no*. You say something different. Every several years, something different. And I try. I flow into it. I take deep roots, which will grow in time. But my heart, the word that stuck, that I can project and internalize, feed to my inner voice, my personal history is at rest.

****

As an adult, I know I'm out. I have a wife. I still wonder if I'm gay. Despite the orgasms and rises in emotion. The tenderness me and my wife have. The warmth when another same-for-same butch couple passes us by. Still, other women look like me. Other women in this small town I'm not originally from look like me. Though my gaydar is bad, warped to say the least, and my eyes go buggy at slight tendencies, I know that they are not gay. They are not me, even if life is not a lie for them. That I will never know.

I bought Carhartt sweatshirts from an online store when I moved to the somewhat small rural town I live in. I thought, this is great. Those urban kids in Brooklyn are wearing them as fashionable, and I just might also get away with the look while traveling. The urban kids must know, as I know, that they really are of superior quality, rugged, well-sewn, and particularly comfortable. It is the best held rural secret.

The Carhartt sweatshirts helped me fit in at auctions. I owe them a long life, numerous washes. With less to do in rural areas, you branch out, find strange hobbies, get into the nooks and crannies of the place. Here, I found auctions and the bold display of others' used junk up for sale. My wife and I took an interest in antique 78 RPM records. We would buy, gather, and resell. Auctions sell the things, almost always at the end of a long day, at a particularly low cost.

Auctions are dusty. They smell faintly of aged plastic from toys and moldy paper. A kitchen is always cooking egg sandwiches and selling slices of pie and cake early in the day. Cans of soda might be fifty cents. The men gather, Carhartt clad, in small groups and discuss the politics, local misgivings.

They collaborate, say who will bid on what.

I'm in the corner, watching them chat. I've made three or four friends. My Carhartt sweatshirt blends me in all too well. They might adjust and look, clear their throat and stare, or nod once directly. But no one is sure. My disguise is too good in this place with several other women, rough and tumble, sweatshirts of their own, jeans with a few holes, though often a man at their side.

These are the auctions of my neighboring towns. These people are all around me, and I'm safe.

****

My wife has much better gaydar than I do, that's for sure. She grew up in a rural area, out in the country, and doesn't have to find her place in this new, small town. Picking lesbians out here like I pick lesbians out in a city is second nature to her. She must love this place because she knows it. I love the town I see as a mystique.

We were on a bike ride months ago. A woman sat on a bench where we parked our car. Her head perked up as we approached.

"Excuse me." She used polite language and paused and waited, held me waiting, until my wife also caught up and dismounted. "Are you two a gay couple?"

I stumbled for words.

"Yes. Yes. We are," my wife said.

How else would we meet? Would we break through and become friends? With the LGBTQ+ center miles away in the largest city, how would we meet?

We chatted about her partner stuck in a wheelchair and not able to walk the trail with her. Where did she go for help? Who were her friends? We were the same people, in just about the same place. We knew or were starting to know this, her situation. Of course, we would cope. She would be okay because for so many life is.

And if we need a friend, we will ask on the trail or the street. Excuse me, you two, who could be nothing else, are you a gay couple? We can say we are lesbians because someone has asked us.

I encourage you to love a butch, same for same, or otherwise. A Fabergé egg like no other. Their emotion may appear shuttered, or a temper may scare you, but a tenderness will appear, and they will live and die by your side. Find the weak spot. Take a pick to the egg. You will cure ailments and realign stars.

Understanding can live and die. Crack the shell of a glassy eyed, sotic beast. If you see me on the street, I'm open for platonic friendship— tomboy, soft butch, and nonbinary souls preferred. I give a decent haircut. Just ask.

Authentically Butch
By Gabby Cohen

I have always been drawn to masculinity. When I was a kid it presented for me in being a tomboy, a phase I was assured that I would grow out of once I hit puberty. Laughter ensues. When I did hit puberty, my AFAB peers started getting interested in boys and makeup, and I couldn't relate. I remember a school field trip to the fairgrounds in sixth grade. The girls in the car with me were doing their hair and makeup, and confused by this, I said. "What are you doing? We are going to the fair! It's dusty and dirty and we are going to ride rides and hang out with farm animals, why would you get all pretty?" And they looked at me, shook and confused, and said, "Uh, because there will be *boys* there and we want to look good, duh!"

That was the first moment I can remember that familiar feeling of not fitting in. I was happy for a chance to be rugged and dirty, to have an excuse to wear more masculine clothes without question. I would undoubtedly come home dirty and sweaty and nobody would question why I wanted to wear shorts and a T-shirt. As a very queer, very butch, non-binary person everything was isolating. I truly couldn't relate to any of my peers.

My queer identity was the first one I found, when I was fourteen, I thought at the time, that it helped everything make sense. Oh, okay, I didn't get it because I don't like boys, now it makes sense. And for a while, it did. It gave a lot of leeway and permission to not be quite as feminine, or to be a little different. It was a safe little bubble for me to be a little weird and quirky in. My cishet family and friends were able to write things off as, well, it's different but that's okay because Gabby is a lesbian!

But as it happens, I still wasn't quite right. Par for the course when you find an identity and finally start to try it on, other parts of your authentic self start to come into place. So my butch identity kept trying to come out. People in my life seemed to draw a line though, I pushed their comfort levels too much.

Gay? Okay, we can handle that. Masculine? Wait wait now too far, too much.

The comments were always, *you can't wear that, you look like a man, why would you want to dress like a man?, sir, you're going into the wrong bathroom, being gay isn't an excuse to dress sloppy, you're still a girl, nobody is going to find you attractive if you dress like that.*

Being out in the early 2000s was scary enough, I realized very quickly that attraction to masculine presentation needed to get shelved really quickly. It felt like whenever I tried to dive into more masculine presentation, I found that not only did I not fit in CisHet land, I also didn't fit in my queer community. Comments about being butch or a dyke were all derogatory.

If you dress like a man they will all think you want to be one, and we just can't have that.

We've worked too hard to come this far, this sets us back

You have to embrace your womanhood.

The raging feminist in me was like Okay! You are right, I have to do this to fight for us all! And so that identity just went back on the shelf, collecting dust.

It wasn't until I was in my early thirties that I finally was ready and able to take that identity off the shelf, for real this time, and as it turns out for good. I finally started to allow myself to explore my masculinity. And step by step, I started to come into myself. I bought clothes that I liked, that fit my body. I bought the boots I would only ever daydream about wearing. I finally started carrying a pocketknife. I started going to a barbershop for haircuts so I could get a fresh fade. Along the way I've found other butch buddies who have similar experiences and found out I wasn't so alone after all.

After all this time, I finally feel at home in myself. I finally feel safe and seen. I finally am able to just be myself, as authentically as possible. Living in my authenticity helped me find my wife and kid, my chosen family, a handsome butch community, and most of all, myself.

Butch 4 Butch
By Beck Guerra Carter

You're a wonder
Butch brother
Plaid and leather
The piercing
In your crooked smile
You laugh across
The table from me
And I love you so much
In this moment
I wish I could taste
Your buzzcut
Your arm is tethered
Around your wife
And that's fine
I have mine to think of
But I allow myself this gaze
And think about
How much I love
Butches
And the people
Who love them

On Being a Butch Creator
By Missouri Vaun

For the first story I wrote as a romance writer, I imagined a time when being gay is as unquestioned and un-judged as having blue eyes. Some might label my debut novel, *All Things Rise*, as fantasy or science fiction, but I'd like to think of it as the future.

I had a lot of fun writing a story where being gay is openly accepted. I think it was also very therapeutic. My characters didn't feel anxious while holding their lover's hands in public. Nor did they feel the need to femme up or masc down. The uneasiness and hyper alertness that often comes with being a gender outlaw and sexual minority were nonexistent in this world. They were free to just be. As a butch lesbian creator of such a setting, I appreciated it even more.

There were no bathrooms off limits in this fictional world. I instead gifted myself a mental retreat from the fervid gender gatekeepers of public restrooms across the United States. Many of whom I have unfortunately encountered on the West Coast, where I live, despite its progressive reputation. My characters did not have to navigate any of this hostility, or what many of us just call queer problems. What's more, *my* characters never have to. As a creator, I can build whatever universes come to my mind, and my mind never tires of conjuring up stories full of butch heroes, protagonists, and love interests. All of the stories many of us would have loved to read when we were younger but never could. I certainly couldn't.

Growing up lesbian, and a butch lesbian at that, in the Deep South sometimes cast me as a stranger in my own world. I was raised Southern Baptist and my upbringing in that particular faith practice definitely had an impact on me. They certainly don't call the Deep South the Bible Belt for nothing. Funny thing is, intuitively I knew this, but I began to think of this differently when I began writing love stories. Perhaps because the worlds and characters I imagined were not reminiscent of any of the worlds I had experienced growing up. I suppose every writer probably realizes that at some point and I suppose I am no different. But I see now how this personal experience of navigating as an outsider for so many years informs the motivations of many of the characters that populate my stories. Like all of us, many of my characters are longing to belong and not just in a superficial way, but in an authentic and meaningful way. That begins when we truly accept who we are.

For starters, there are women who look like me in my books. What a concept! Some may even call it revolutionary. For far too many of our queer ancestors, that was sadly not the case. But it's still a struggle even today with the resurgence of book bans across the country. Books with LGBTQ characters continue to be some of the most banned books in the United States and around the world. But thanks to publishers such as Bold Strokes Books and literary advocates such as Lambda Literary and the Golden Crown Literary Society, more of us are seeing ourselves on the page, and it's amazing. Our experiences are finally being validated, our insecurities, our hurts, and our hangups, just like the fully dimensional human beings that we are. We're also getting to enjoy idealized versions of ourselves as well through courageous wildfire fighters, world-saving scientists, and daredevil stunt drivers, just to describe a few of my characters. Although I know for sure there are real-life lesbians mastering these arenas.

What's more, my butch lesbians are the main characters of my stories. They are not relegated to the sidelines to be ridiculed for the toxic male hetero gaze nor are they props to seductively tease the righteous female hetero gaze. My butch lesbians are fully realized characters who have their own lives and are not interested in appeasing anyone except themselves and their romantic desires, which are often satiated after a slow burn journey they don't fully understand until they do. I'm a romance writer after all.

Which segues to another element of my stories: you can always count on a Missouri Vaun story to have beautiful women who challenge the primary butch character's blind spots, and vice versa. My main protagonists, like all of us, are learning about themselves all of the time. Sometimes a bad breakup gets us in a rut. Other times, the residual fear from traumatic events holds us back. Or we simply just need an extra launch boost to adulting. Whatever it may be, my main protagonists are on some kind of journey to self-discovery, and ultimately to true love, which helps get them there faster. Well, that's how it looks on the surface. If you read closer, you'll see that the women embarking on the slow burn journey together are helping each other figure out what they need to figure out in order to get to the next level of their overall life path. Sounds heavy, but don't worry. There's a lot of making out and sex in between. I've learned as a romance writer that healing yourself through love takes a lot of kissing.

There's also a lot of drama. What is life without it? Miscommunication? Check. Broken hearts? Check. Self-sabotage? Check. Awful exes? Check. In conjunction with lots of adventure, big and small, to bring my main characters together. From lost dogs and road trips to natural disasters and apocalyptic saves, I got our queer storylines covered.

All in all, I suppose we each want what my characters want— to find our place in the world and to feel content once we've discovered that place. That's a real struggle for many of us, especially members of the LGBTQ community. It's harder if you've never seen anyone like yourself accomplish this. For far too long our books and movies had tragic endings. That's because for far too long, many of our lives were often tragic. They weren't easy. That's why our histories deserve to be celebrated now more than ever. Despite it all, we still persevered, and managed to find our pockets of queer joy. In addition to writing everyday stories and timely science fiction, I've written a good number of historical romances with butch protagonists as well.

Crossing The Wide Forever takes place in the United States of the mid-1800s. Slavery and massacres were prevalent during this time period and gravely impacted the lives of Black and Indigenous women. Many White women dressed as men to migrate west to flee abusive relationships or to avoid unwanted marriage arrangements. When I read about this, my butch heart instantly gravitated toward all the butch stories out there. Many White women during this time had two options, get married or do sex work to survive. The third, more radical option was to dress as a man and find work. Only men had the luxury of finding decent paying jobs out west. I read tons of personal accounts and did tons of research for my own personal interests, and to put the reader in Cody and Lillie's world. *Crossing The Wide Forever* is about adventure, about charting your own course, about believing in yourself, and ultimately about falling in love.

Whiskey Sunrise takes place a bit more recently. It is the story of Lovey Porter and Royal Duval in Prohibition-era Georgia of the 1920s. This narrative is by far the most personal story I have written. My great-grandfather was a Church of God minister and a moonshiner and saw no conflict between those two pursuits. And as I mentioned before, I grew up in the Deep South, and wrestled with my Baptist faith and my sexuality, and oftentimes felt very alone. The love story between Lovey and Royal reflects many of the challenges I faced growing up queer in the Bible Belt. My faith was such a part of me, but so was my queerness and butchness. They were all a part of me. No one should be forced to hide an integral part of themselves. I tried until I couldn't. Despite the initial pain, I was better for it, and thankfully love won again. *Whiskey Sunrise* is about that journey that so many of us have to take, and the love that awaits all of us.

Writing is such a solitary event. Yet, the stories we create touch so many lives. I am honored to be a part of this sacred tradition. I've received lots of emails and social media posts over the years, and they all seem to point to the same sentiment. That my writing makes people feel better. That kind of feedback is invaluable, and it makes me feel like what I'm doing matters. Perhaps in the near future, being a butch woman, nonbinary, or trans, will be as unquestioned and unjudged as having blue eyes. If my stories had anything to do with it, count me honored.

Summer Solstice Sunsets
By Jen T. Stoughton

There's something to sunsets seen from a rooftop. They're somehow redder, more bruise-like and summery than those seen from street level. And there's a breathless quality to them, too, like the air's been sucked from the top of the atmosphere, specks of stars spread in its place. The air below is softer, cloudy with everyone's breath pushed up against each other's and muffled as if under a blanket. Up here it's still, and clear, and aching.

I've been up here with Joan a couple of times, and I've come to understand how addicting the tall twilight air can be. And how dangerous. Not for the reasons my mother warns me I shouldn't be up there, like *I'll catch my wintry death* or *the fall could break my back* or *my nice new skirt will get soiled.* It's because the air is so aching-clear and still that it holds an edge, high-altitude sharp. If you move the wrong way, you can cut yourself open. The sky itself holds you still in its fist.

Like Joan's still, right now. I should take a picture. Restless Joan Harris, caffeine in human form, Joan Harris, physically-couldn't-sit-still-if-her-life-depended-on-it Joan Harris, sitting there at the edge of the roof with her feet dangling into the thick light below. No one would believe me if I told them. The wind toys at her short hair, but otherwise she seems frozen in time. Joan stares at the sun, maybe going blind. I stare at Joan, maybe going blind.

I feel like I should look away. We came up here—well, Joan grabbed me by the wrist and dragged me up, more like—because Joan read online somewhere that summer solstice sunsets are the most breathtaking of all, and decided we needed the best view in the city to appreciate it properly. I should stop looking at Joan and determine for myself if it's true. I should look at the sky.

City skies aren't beautiful. They're half blocked by steel and concrete, half clogged with smoke and life and dirt. I don't see what all the birds are so fussed about. Sometimes I wonder if the sky has actually been scraped up by the high-reaching buildings—even on clear blue days there's something broken about it, scarred.

Breaks and scars aren't beautiful. I've been to museums, I took art history. I've seen the way the paint blends smoothly into itself, seen the gold and the green of nature and how the softness of people is lovingly rendered. I've seen the marble statues, chipped at until sharp edges run together like satin, silk, skin. Those are artworks—masterpieces because they're flat, and calm, and quiet. Especially the women, they're all serene, almost asleep. My mother always told me that good girls kept their hands folded, ankles crossed, mouths shut. Even though Venus was completely nude, looking at her made me think of that. Eyes down, lips sealed. Pretty.

My art teacher loved the Romantic paintings, where the people looked just as noble and perfect as the landscapes behind them. She went on and on about how much passion they displayed, how much life and movement each image held. All I saw was their silence.

If Joan weren't Joan, she'd look a little like some of those paintings now. With the sky behind her fading into all sorts of colors and her head outlined by the setting sun, she could almost be any of those nobly perfect heroes frozen in her moment of quiet triumph. Like she's pressed up against glass between one breath and the next, heart beating into canvas. Beautiful.

But breaks and scars aren't beautiful.

Joan's got scars like the night's got constellations. The sun's moved a bit so now I can make out the one by her ear, another slashing through her eyebrow. My eyes want to trace where I know others lay—sluggishly crawling across a hip-bone, darting across broad shoulders, ripping into a knee—but at the same time, my eyes don't really want to leave her face. It's always been easy for me to rest my gaze there. *Maybe I'll start wearing grooves with my stares*, I think. *Maybe I already have.* Maybe I'll get to leave a mark on Joan Harris.

But marks and blemishes aren't beautiful.

But Joan is anyway.

Joan's sunset-beautiful, breathless and sharp and bruise-purple-red. She takes *peace and quiet* between her teeth and cracks them like sunflower seeds, spitting them off the roof with a crooked grin. She lets her trousered legs splay open and her cackle echo in her wide-open mouth. She's wild, is what she is, and joyous with it. She's—

She's looking at me, now, while I'm still looking at her. A breeze picks at her hair again but the space between us stands still.

"Whatcha doin' over there?" she calls to me, almost casual, nearly hoarse. Who knows how long we've been sitting here in the silence she's just broken.

"Painting you with my eyes," I reply without thinking. I can't think around her, sometimes. "With words."

And the sun sets again in Joan's eyes just then, flares gold. "Do I make a pretty picture?"

Pretty dumb, that's for sure is the teasing reply on the tip of my tongue, the one I'd give down on the ground, but I swallow it. "You're too much to be a picture," is what comes out, true and all the more painful for it. "You can't be captured in just two dimensions."

"That sounds like a confession," Joan says in warning. Suddenly I know we're on the edge of this. This *this* that's dangerous and difficult and only has a slim chance of leaving either of us happy. But the rooftop air is sharp in my lungs and the light is fading and Joan is *beautiful*.

"Maybe it is," I say.

Joan's got a scar that cuts through her bottom lip. It tastes like a promise.

Butch
By Rebecca Ritts

I fell in love with her swagger, her T-shirts with the arms ripped off, her tattoos, her work boots.

I fell in love with the way she looked in her baseball cap and sunglasses.

I fell in love with the way she got out of her truck.

I fell in love with her quiet confidence, and the gentle teddy bear she was when we were alone together.

I fell in love with her blue, blue eyes.

The way her jeans fit, slightly tight across her hips and back side but loose everywhere else.

I fell in love with the way she wrote and then later, the way she talked.

I fell in love with the way she wooed me with her words.

The way she would call me out of the blue just to tell me she was thinking of me.

The way she would sigh when we were talking on the phone to each other.

I fell in love with the gentle bantering and flirtatiousness we couldn't seem to stop no matter how hard we tried.

I fell in love with her crooked grin and the twinkle in her eye, which let me know exactly what she was thinking.

I fell in love with her for all of the romantic gestures she would bestow upon me.

I fell in love with the way she didn't take shit from anyone.

I fell in love with her commitment to her family.

I fell in love with her loyalty to her friends.

I fell in love with her boxer briefs. And what was underneath.

I fell in love with the way people would sometimes mistake her for a man, and they would get flustered but she didn't.

I fell in love with the way she held my hand.

I fell in love with the way she offered me a Hershey's Kiss in a dark theater.

I fell in love with the way she showed her appreciation of my perfume and black velvet dress.

I fell in love with the way she moved. With the way she kissed.
I fell in love with her even more when my family grew to love her.

I fell in love with her even more for the relationship she has with my mother.

I fell in love with her even more for the parent she became to my children.

I fell in love with her even more when she stood by my side no matter what came our way.

Quaintly Queer
By Kristin Schloemer

What does being butch mean to me? Oh, so many things. My mind immediately races and my heart beats faster, thinking of all the ways my butch, soft butch, to clarify, identity is intertwined into so many areas of my life. I haven't always loved this part of me but every day I'm learning to embrace all that I am. In no particular order, here is what being butch means to me.

A stomachache. The kind you get when you like someone, the nervousness, the attraction. Butterflies. A stomachache. The kind you get when you feel fear or are scared. When you are trying to convince yourself that something is not as bad as it really is or when you're anticipating disappointment or anger.

Warm on the inside. When I walk by a cute girl and our eyes meet. A spark is felt throughout my body, a smirk comes to my face and I immediately become aware of my presence, how I'm walking, how I look, making sure this cute girl knows I've noticed. A little bit of confidence and a little bit of swagger.

Being butch means that she gets to be the feminine one. This is not to say that I'm not feminine at times but I feel good bringing more masculine energy to a relationship. I'm drawn to a certain femininity a woman can have, the way she moves, the softness and curves of her body that complement the slight roughness and flat land that is my body.

It means I will give you my jacket if you're cold and I'll open doors for you, trying to remember to let you go in first. I will put my hand on your leg as I'm driving and remind you the Jeep needs an oil change. I will touch your lower back or butt when I walk by, just because.

It means being patient and making sure you're comfortable being with me. Checking in with you frequently to make sure you are doing ok. It means I keep you safe. I hold you physically and sexually safe, be open and understanding so you feel emotionally safe, let you take the lead on things at a pace you feel is right for you. It feels like I have a responsibility to make sure my girl is taken care of. I love how this feels.

Feeling alone. Getting bullied in school, my family home and cars vandalized, unaccepting family, losing friends, low self-esteem and confidence, physically assaulted and mentally and verbally abused. Keeping secrets. Isolated from those who are designed to be there for you, accept you, love you. Thoughts of self-harm and suicide. Depression. Anxiety. Anger.

Feeling lost and misunderstood. I didn't have everything figured out at fifteen years old. I'm not sure I have things figured out now. I didn't know how to verbalize what I was thinking and feeling but when I didn't hear anyone else talking about being attracted to another girl, I felt like no one understood what was happening.

Butch to me means that I try and fix things or figure out the electronics in the house and that if we were on the Titanic, I would insist that you take the whole door for yourself….after you've let me draw you like one of my French girls.

It means that I find comfort and familiarity in love stories like this because I so deeply can resonate with chivalry and the ways your heart feels like it could explode when the girl loves you. Take care of your girl, worship her body and mind, set her on fire.

Anxious. Feeling like I can never really forget how others see me. I can't hide. I am the stereotypical butch lesbian, soft butch, to clarify. Many times I feel like I'm outed before I even open my mouth. This isn't necessarily a bad thing but being butch feels like I'm always on.

That feeling when you finally find a professional that cuts your short hair to perfection. Haircut day is a *very* big deal.

Shopping in the men's section for clothes or shoes. Feeling comfortable with myself but having the common occurrence of someone staring or talking to the person next to them. I don't shop in this section of the store because I want to be a man. Not at all. I shop in the men's section because this is how I feel comfortable, this is what I think looks good on my body, this is part of what I think is sexy and appealing to the women I'm interested in. Remember, she gets to wear the dress or the heels or the makeup. So beautiful.

Being butch means that I make sure to create an environment where she trusts me and knows I have her best interests in mind. It means that I press closer into her when I feel her breath catch when we kiss, wrap my arms around her while she's still shaking and wipe her tears.

I am the big spoon. The end.

Some of the butch rules— always smell good, shirt matches your socks, belt matches your shoes, it's sexy when the waistband from my boxer brief trunks sits on top of my jeans that rest on my hip bones, you wear a beater every day, you tip the waitresses well, be a cock block for your friends and the best guy friend to them that's not actually a guy.

Being butch means getting called out in a female restroom, even though I intentionally walk in a way that would, or should, accentuate what little chest I do have. It means that the more comfortable I feel with myself, sometimes the more uncomfortable others feel with who I am. Fuck them. I'm so tired of feeling like how I look, how I act, how I present myself is somehow wrong or uncomfortable for others. Being butch means you exist, even when others tell you you're doing it wrong.

I will carry all of your belongings when you decide you don't want to carry your purse or wallet. Don't worry, I have more than enough pockets in these shorts.

At some point in life, as a butch, soft butch, to clarify, I get the amazing opportunity to share clothes with my son. Need a sweater? Shirt? Boom. Double the wardrobe for both of us!

Wink at the girls but only when you mean it. A small yet personal gesture that lets her know that she's special. Slick.

Being butch means I have big feelings but I feel I should try and keep it together. I am not always successful at this.

Sometimes being butch means it can be more difficult to know what to do with feelings that are traditionally considered feminine, being comfortable showing others the softer sides you keep hidden or fear you will be judged for.

It means sometimes people forget that I'm still a woman and I have to remind them that I'm more than the assumptions they are making based on my appearance.

Being butch means that my relationship and family are just as valid as yours.

Seeing another butch in public and exchanging the *nod*.

Blushing when a girl hits on you. Blushing and walking a little taller when a girl hits on you and not him.

Sometimes feeling like you don't fully fit in with women but you also don't feel like you fully fit in with men.

You make sure the girls are treated right by others. You're protective.

You want to be taken seriously with your butch, soft butch, to clarify, identity. Accept me for who I am.

For me, being butch means I don't particularly like the word lesbian but in the right circumstance, from the right person, queer could feel okay.

You do not deserve and will not get an apology from me because you don't like who I am.

Heartache. When you lose family, friends, opportunities or jobs, just for being who you are. When your heart breaks because someone is telling you that you're wrong.

Strength. Being butch means that I will come out to others countless times in my life, sometimes without my consent. There is pride and allure in being both. My combination of masculine and feminine, butch and femme, beautiful and handsome works for me, very well.

Love. Finding people who look like me, act like me, feel things like I do is unbelievably comforting and reassuring. When you feel like you've found your people and are accepted and celebrated.

Being butch means I need to impress her parents, show them that even though I'm not a guy, I'm still a good choice for their daughter.

It can mean that people can be uncomfortable by the idea I could find a male attractive or not take this seriously.

It means I'm not taken seriously when it comes to having children, especially the idea of me being pregnant.

It means that I still think my family is disappointed/hurt/embarrassed that I'm not only gay but butch, also.

Being butch means that I have a hard time getting served at the bar. I don't look like the women that society would categorize as pretty, attractive, sexy. I find that the type of bar doesn't really matter. In my experience, traditionally beautiful and sexy women will likely get served first.

My identity as butch, soft butch, to clarify, feels very quaint to me. It can feel small or unusual at times but there is safety and familiarity in this that feels like home. I feel respectful and old-fashioned in the way I try to treat women. It's important to me. This intimate part of me is in everything I am and I'm proud of that. Plus, the ladies fucking love it.

Being butch means that I want someone to hold me and tell me that everything is going to be okay much more often than I express. Sometimes I want you to take charge, emotionally, physically, sexually. Sometimes I want to be handled. Help me feel comfortable in being vulnerable with you.

"I feel there is something unexplored about women that only a woman can explore." -Georgia O'Keeffe

Being butch means I can be trusted with your mind, body and heart. Invite me in? Let me see you, feel you, hear you, taste you. Let me experience all of you and show you just how much I love, want and need you.

It means that I will always worry how my children will be treated because of how I'm perceived by others. I desperately want them to be proud of me and our family.

Being butch means learning to be okay losing people, being a topic of conversation, the focus of the humor but it also means learning to be okay with who I am, what I stand for, how I love and what makes me happy.

An Insider's Guide on How to Properly Appreciate a Butch
By Rae Theodore

Run your hands over her velvety head after she gets her hair buzzed.

Let her know how much it turns you on when she wears her baseball cap backward.

Tell her that her necktie makes her eyes sparkle.

Keep your hands off her hair gel, tools, and copy of *Fun Home*.

Own at least one skirt with a really long slit.

Never tell anyone that she always cries while watching *A League of Their Own*.

Pretend to be riveted by her old softball/field hockey/basketball/gym class stories, even though you've heard them all before.

Replace the word cute with handsome when complimenting her. For example, that's a handsome hat or you look handsome in that jacket.

Insist that she should have been cast as Shane in *The L Word*.

Don't make a big fuss when she wears her dressy T-shirt to that event you're attending.

Let her open the door for you despite the fact that you are a capable independent woman.

Let her carry your bags.

Trace her scars, the ones you can see and the ones you can't, with your fingertips when you're lying in bed at night.

Tell her she's beautiful until she believes it, even though she's never felt beautiful a day in her life.

Before the Slumber Party
By Xequina Ma. Berber

I didn't have any friends my first year in high school. I felt like I was invisible, but that was actually good because I lugged around the weight of a deep, dark secret. I was doing okay academically, but the locker room experience was traumatic because I was so afraid girls would guess what I was. Like an anorexic in a candy store, I kept my eyes to myself, performed the gym rituals of showering and changing, and got out of there again as fast as I could.

Close to the end of that school year my sister Luisa, a popular senior, had a slumber party. On the designated night, she was downstairs, already in her night gown, helping my mother prepare snacks. The doorbell rang, and it was Mayra, hours early, with a round overnight case and a big purse. She started talking as soon as I opened the door.

"Oh, hi Toni, sorry I'm so early. Chris had to drop me off because he has a swim meet. Is your sister home?" I didn't have a chance even to say hi because Luisa came out and took over and they jabbered at each other, saying stuff like *Omigod, I have so much to tell you!* and everything.

Mayra was my sister's best friend and just as popular. With her long straight hair and thick-lashed, hazel eyes, she was the quintessential sixties girl. My sister, not so much. Both of them were cool though, unlike me. Our family was friends with Mayra's family. We met them at the Dominican college church in Berkeley and got together a lot. They loved my mom's Mexican cooking.

I was pals with her brother, Chris, also in high school. After those family dinners Chris and I would go out to the back of the garden with his cigarettes and a beer if I could sneak one. We'd talk about surfing and motorcycles, and everyone teased us about puppy love. I let them think that. I even had his class picture in my wallet, in case I ever got asked if I had a boyfriend. But the couple of times we tried kissing it was gross, like kissing warm, wet cardboard. I think it was the same for him, which was just as well.

With nothing to do and my sister telling me I was in the way in the kitchen, I wandered upstairs. Mayra was in the bathroom, I could hear music from her transistor radio, *this magic moment, so different and—"*

Sometimes, when she wasn't around, I'd go into my sister's room and look at the pink and white panties and bras in her dresser drawer, which looked huge to me since Luisa was developed, a quasi-incestuous secret pastime. Mayra's purse was on a chair, I'd looked in that before, so I made a beeline for the overnight case, wide open on the bed. It was black patent leather with a loop handle, lined in a pink fabric with tiny white rosebuds and a gathered pocket on the inside lid.

There was a white polka-dot nightgown in the suitcase—Swiss dot. We had curtains made of the stuff—right on top. A pink ribbon attached to the case, held everything in place with a neat little bow on top. I smelled roses. I ran my hand over the nightgown, soft and light as snow. With one finger, I pulled out the pocket on the lid and looked inside: washcloth, toothbrush and tube of toothpaste, a bottle of Tea Rose eau de Cologne.

Before my sister got into high school and was too cool to hang out with me, she found a spooky green book on witchcraft at Holmes Book Company, an antiquarian bookstore downtown Oakland. My sister and I would meet in a basement room for a late-night snack of hors d'oeuvre creations we made of odds and ends from the refrigerator. I'd put on an old velveteen Halloween witch hat my mother had made, and Luisa an old fuzzy black fingertip cape our aunt had given her. We'd sneak down to the basement room, light a candle, and Luisa would tell me what she was learning from the book. Ceremonially, she assembled things like a silver spoon, wine glasses, a little porcelain lady whose big skirt hid a bell, and herbs—some dried from our pantry, some picked fresh, like mint. Then we chanted spells for her to get the angora sweater set she wanted, or to shoot a hoop or two at a meet.

"Isn't this a sin though?" I had asked. We were Catholic.

"It's just for fun," Luisa assured me. "And if they work, it probably would have happened anyway. I'm not going to put curses on people. *That* would be a sin. I haven't even read that part of the book." She arranged the cape around her so it flared onto the floor. "Anyway, nobody believes in magic anymore."

She had told me roses were sacred to Aphrodite and had been used in love potions a long time ago. Luisa had a lot of rose-scented things, and probably told Mayra about it. It must work, because they both had lots of boyfriends. I realized now, perfume was a modern-day love potion. Maybe after-shaves were, too.

I listened for Mayra, still in the bathroom, singing to a popular song. I lifted the edge of the nightgown to see what else was in there. Slippers, curlers, a box of Tampax. Tampons were still mysterious and sophisticated. Girls I knew started getting their periods in seventh and eighth grades, and we all used Kotex. The box was open and I was thinking about look-ing inside when I heard the music go off and snatched my hand away. Just in time, because Mayra came in with her radio and a make-up bag.

"What are you doing in here?" She asked like she was really interested. Luisa always kicked me out when her friends were over.

"No-thing," I said, and my stupid voice cracked. I cleared my throat and lowered my voice. "I, uh, like your suit-case." I said it as if that was the reason I was standing there, acting all guilty.

"Thank you. Isn't it boss? It's just like one the Shrimp has."

Jean Shrimpton was the most famous model of the time, with long hair and giant eyes. I knew about her because I was always taking Luisa's Cosmo's to look at pictures of women in underwear. Her magazines were safe reading mate-rial, not like being caught looking at my brother's Playboys, plus I didn't feel as guilty. Luisa didn't mind, and my mom thought I was showing an interest in being a lady someday. I was just waiting to like boys. What was the big hurry was to like guys. I was only fourteen.

"It cost a bundle," Mayra was saying, looking in the mirror and doing something with her bangs. "I asked for it, but my mom said no, then my parents surprised me with it for my birthday."

Mayra had put on a bunch of make-up, which she couldn't do at home. It was weird, since she wasn't going anywhere except to sleep, which probably wouldn't be until one or two. Girls flirt and impress each other with make-up and clothes when guys aren't around. I wondered about that sometimes.

She checked her make-up in the dresser mirror, then got out her blush and put more on. She started talking about her senior ball, which had happened a few weeks earlier.

"Remember Sandy?" She didn't wait for an answer. "She was at my house when you guys came over on Easter."

She took off her dress and folded it up, standing there in a bra and matching panties, and even a garter belt and stockings. Her underwear was peach with lace on the edges, practically sheer. I could see the shadows at the tip of her breasts and the dark patch through her panties. I could feel myself getting red and hot all over, but I couldn't just leave while she was talking.

"Let me show you her picture, you're going to die."

Mayra had barely ever talked to me before, and even though I knew she was just bored, I liked that she was treating me as if I was her friend. She dug her wallet out of her purse. I went and stood next to her as she paged through all her pictures, friends, guys, a dog she used to have. I glimpsed a handmade, heart-shaped amulet with an eye that I knew from that book was supposed to guarantee fidelity. My sister had one just like it. They probably made them together.

"Here."

I remembered Sandy as a dull-faced blonde, but in the snapshot was a transformed, happy-looking Sandy with her boyfriend in someone's living room, hair tied on top of her head with curls and ribbons spilling down the side of her face. She wore a pale pink dress with an airy, layered skirt. A lamp behind her shone through the gauzy ruffles. A wavy, pinkish string of light marred the dress. It was a photographic flaw, but added to her magic, fairy-like appearance.

"Danny broke up with her a week later. She was crushed. They've been together since they were freshmen. We had class pictures taken that week and she couldn't even smile for the camera."

She flipped to another page in her wallet. This one was black and white, polarized, Sandy gazing mournfully upward. She looked like a cherub on someone's grave. Mayra was standing so close I could feel the heat coming off her. Quietly, I sniffed. Sure enough, she was wearing rose perfume. She closed the wallet and put it back in her purse.

"What about *your* senior ball pictures, can I see them?" I asked. I wanted her to go on showing me stuff, but she started taking off her stockings.

"No, they're at home. The guy I was supposed to go with got mono and I had to find someone else to go with at the last minute. I went with this other guy, it was boring, and the pictures were awful. I should have just stayed home."

When Mayra's garter belt and stockings were off, rolled up and tucked into the side of her case, she took off her bra. Her breasts were small and perfect. I felt light-headed and sat down on the bed while she put on her night gown. When she pulled it down over her head, I pretended to be looking at the posters around my sister's room, one a giant poster of the Jefferson Airplane. A photo of Twiggy in psychedelic colors. Sybil Leek, an English witch, hair flying, holding some magic pendulum. Mayra came over and stood in front of me. Her nipples were exactly level with my eyes. She touched my head.

"I can do your hair for you."

I liked to keep my hair short, but I was long overdue for a haircut.

"Sure."

"Come over here."

I was both relieved and sorry not to have her nipples in my face. Standing in front of the dresser mirror, I saw we were just as tall as each other. She started combing my hair. "Don't take this the wrong way, Toni, but you look like a guy. You'd be really cute if you made yourself up."

The comb was hard to use on my thick mop, so she got my sister's brush—Luisa never let anyone touch her precious brush, but I didn't say anything. Mayra brushed most of my hair back, leaving a bunch of bangs. Then she got one of my sister's scarves with roses and pink flowers and tied it head-band style, the knot low on the side, with the ends hanging down. She got my sister's sewing scissors and waste basket. I wondered if Luisa was going to ban me from her room for the rest of my life.

"Okay if I trim your bangs? They're too long. Here," she said, handing me the wastebasket. Hold it under your face while I cut."

I didn't like all this primping stuff, but I was really digging the attention. Plus, I was kind of in a trance, being so close to a girl who wasn't my gross sister. After the bangs, she put purple eye shadow on me, then blush. She could have put horns and a Pinocchio nose on me and I wouldn't have cared. I could see through her nightgown, with only those Swiss dots to distract me, and my eyes were glued to her chest. She caught me staring. I stammered and said the first thing that came to me:

"You—um, Mayra, I, uh, I can see your boobs."

"So? Suffer," she said all sassy. She pulled the nightgown tight over her chest and looked in the mirror. "Lots of women aren't wearing bras anymore. I don't think I need one, but my parents make me wear them. What do you think?" She turned toward me. She was actually giving me permission to look! I was turning all kinds of red and my rolling eyes kept returning to land on her nipples, smashed flat against the practically sheer cloth.

"Uh, uh, I-I don't wear one," I said idiotically.

"Don't. Anyway, you don't need one," she said, and she actually put her hands on my chest! I thought I was going to pass out. "They're so uncomfortable."

She let go of me too soon, and looked through her make-up bag, then opened the drawer to look at Luisa's make-up. She took out a lipstick, grabbed a tissue and wiped off the one she had on. I watched in fascination while she checked herself in the dresser mirror again, then put on the new lipstick.

"This color is *London Rosie*," she said. "I love it, what do you think? But we can't wear the same lipstick, we would look like the Bobbsey Twins."

The *Boobsy* Twins. I inadvertently looked at her breasts again.

She grabbed a tissue from the box on the dresser and blotted her lips, something else girls do that doesn't make sense, leaving a big pink imprint like an open heart on it, then tossing it on the dresser among my sister's perfume bottles. Then Mayra held my chin while she put the lipstick on me. I felt sorry for guys right then. Imagine what it would be like to have a big old dick signaling to the whole world what was in your mind. I looked at myself in the mirror. She had gone over my lip line, and I looked like a little kid who had gotten into her mother's make-up.

She studied me. "That's a good color for you," she said, then she leaned forward and kissed me right on the lips and instinctively, I kissed her back. She giggled and started putting the make-up away, saying how cool Londonderry brand make-up was.

I was reeling. The weird thing was, the kiss seemed like the most natural thing in the world, and at the same time it was so fast, it was almost like it hadn't really happened. But it had. My mouth and heart and *down there* were still throbbing.

The doorbell rang a couple of times but I ignored it. I was having too much fun with Mayra because the kiss had melted my ice and we were saying stuff and teasing each other, like me taking off the scarf and her yelling *hey, put that back on*, which ending up in a pillow fight and jumping up on the bed to get away from each other. That scene lasted about five whole minutes before more girls came in, Luisa behind them, and beyond a glare from her, I was forgotten.

My sister didn't kick me out, probably because mom said I had to be included in the slumber party. I sat at the top of the bed not really listening to all the gab because my brain was going fifty miles an hour: *Why did Mayra kiss me? Did she somehow* know? *Did she secretly like girls too? Had everything been leading up to it, and I was too dense to notice?*

I stared at Mayra, but she was caught up in the gossip. After a while the girls started changing into their nightgowns, but I was too in love to stay and sightsee. I staggered to my room and put on my brother's hand-me-down pajamas. I felt like I did after drinking beer.

I didn't rejoin the girls. Instead I went out to the end of the garden, where I closed my eyes and kissed my hand, reliving the experience, only slowly. Lipstick came off on the back of my hand, I could still smell tea rose, and I kissed myself again and again, pretending Mayra and I were making out and she was feeling my chest again. I fantasized that she liked me more than my sister, that she was going to be my girlfriend, and taking her, dressed like an angel, to the sophomore dance next year.

But those thoughts were soon ruined by reality. Even if I wore Londonderry makeup every day, I wouldn't be cool enough for her. She dated college men, so I was too young for her. Besides, how would we hide our relationship from everyone, especially my sister, who saw everything with her big eyes? Lesbianism was not only illegal, it was a big sin.

By the time I went back inside, my parents were in the den watching TV and Luisa's friends had taken over the living room with their sleeping bags and snacks. I found a place close to Mayra and unrolled my sleeping bag. She turned once, gave me an annoyed look, then ignored me. The girls talked about boys, told dirty jokes I didn't get but laughed at anyway, passed around a slam book my sister made with questions on each page for people to answer, like *What do you think guys talk about when they're together?* Among the notations of *Cars, Beer,* and *Screwing girls!* I wrote, *Who cares?*

The next morning I woke up before anyone else. Eleven girls in sleeping bags in the living room, all the furniture pushed to the sides, popcorn littering the floor. I crawled over to gaze at Mayra. She opened her eyes.

"Stop looking at me," she said crossly, and rolled over.

I grabbed my sleeping bag and took it down to the basement. *Had she noticed that I'd been staring at her all evening?* I got dressed and walked in the cold clear air of morning to eight o'clock mass, thinking about everything that had happened the night before. My smart sister had told me when you're in a relationship, it was important to pay attention to what guys did more than what they said. Of course I'd only been in a relationship for a half hour or so, but I thought it might still count.

That kiss had been the most momentous thing that happened to me since Holy Communion, but obviously hadn't meant anything to Mayra. She had ignored me once my sister and her friends had showed up. I didn't really believe she liked girls. Lesbians were big, strong women who worked at men's jobs, smoked cigars, and could beat up men. There was a bar downtown near the bus station where they hung out, smoking and getting rowdy. Passing them once, my dad had muttered *dykes.* I tried to imagine Mayra with one of them.

With one of *us,* I realized.

So, last night's experience was all mine. If she even remembered doing it, I knew Mayra wouldn't tell my sister, who'd only say it was gross and that Mayra was weird. I hid the memory inside my heart, to take out and cherish whenever I wanted. I'd only been in love for one evening, so I wasn't heartbroken. I felt very mature.

After church I went over to a friend's house I'd had in grammar school and we ate cereal and played monopoly. By the time I got home all the girls were gone and the house was clean, as if there'd never been a slumber party with screaming girls all over the place. My sister was in a bad mood because she'd had to do all the cleaning by herself and yelled at me for letting Mayra use her stuff.

"Your stupid hairs were all over the place, I had to move everything and wipe down my dresser and vacuum. You can empty my wastebasket, and don't touch my stuff again."

I smilingly did as she ordered, not to piss her off, but because thinking about the evening was almost better than having lived it.

The next day at school I walked around thinking *I kissed one of the coolest girls in school! I kissed a senior!* Grinning and being friendly without realizing it, saying hi to anyone who looked at me. My lab partner in biology asked if I had any plans for the summer, and we exchanged phone numbers to go swimming. I even teased girls in Home Ec, pretending like I was going to put detergent and Tabasco in the cake we were making.

I passed Mayra in the hallway. She gave me a quick, quirky smile, like she remembered very well what had happened and knew the effect she had on me. But that could have been my imagination.

I wasn't worrying what people might be thinking about me and I wasn't even uptight in the locker room. I played ball better than ever, my teammates cheering me and slapping me on the back. I had felt sort of confident, even popular that day. Maybe it had something to do with a tissue with a pink *London Rosie* kiss on it, which I had put in my wallet like a secret love amulet.

Bruised
By JD Voss

My summer began early enough, as far as the women were concerned. I had my stables full enough to handle without wearing myself thin. Three women in my hometown was enough for me to handle, for the summer at least. They would offer me the variety I needed, or so I thought. Later, however, I was finding myself increasingly more bored with them and the routine that had begun to develop. Monotony, or monogamy for that matter, was not for me. I craved a change, and fast. So when my best friend Doug offered me the idea of a road trip from Chicago to Indianapolis to hook up with some Myspace chick, I jumped at the chance to break my cycle of boredom. New city, new women, and best of all new connections.

It had been a while since Doug and I spent any quality time together. We met at work, our birthdays are a day apart. He's my road dog, my drinking buddy. He and I have picked up more women together and seen and heard each other fuck every one of them. This was going to be a wild and hopefully wet weekend. I was looking forward to it, I missed my wingman.

Once we hit the road I figured that we would only take a few minutes to catch other each up on life, men can be so unsocial and vague. Our conversation took all of about twenty minutes and he was out like a light. That left me alone with my thoughts. I couldn't help but feel the familiar yearning that always seems to creep over me whenever I visit a new place. The excitement of traveling, seeing new things, a taste of something different. The thrill of being fresh meat in an unknown lesbian world. Don't get it twisted. I'm not a player or a dog for that matter, at least not in my opinion. I just like to enjoy new connections, as I like to call them.

We arrived in Indy and found our way to Markell, Doug's hookup. Good thing we met her at her job, otherwise they would have fucked the second their eyes met. But instead we talked and got to know her a little before she got off work.

Once back to her apartment, the bedroom door shut, the music came on, and the bed creaks began.

I found my way to the room I called mine for the weekend. A twin sized bed with a blanket that had a tiger on it, a few shelves and a small window with nothing much to see outside but a bush. I threw my stuff onto the floor, grabbed a beer from the fridge and joined Markell's two kittens on the couch for a movie. Her cats and I quickly bonded. We all liked beer, movies, and we helped each other to stay distracted from the noises escaping the bedroom. As I tuned out the background noise, my mind wandered from the movie to what adventure might be in store for me that evening.

I had done a little research on what gay things there are to do in this small town. I had heard of this bar called The Ten, the only lesbian bar in Indy. I mean if I'm going to be in Indiana, I might as well see what the lesbians here are all about. I was looking forward to having a few drinks in a new place to observe different women. What would Indy women be like? Would they think I'm cute? Would I step outside my shyness and talk to anyone? All of a sudden I heard the bedroom door slam open and the smell of fresh sex wafted into the air. In ran Doug, wide-eyed with a big smile on his face. I met him with a high-five – my boy had done his work!

Doug and I have known each other long enough and well enough to read each other's eyes—I knew he was into her. I was so happy for him as he had been looking for a girlfriend for a while, or at least a good fuck. When Doug and I went out back in Chicago, straight bars and all, the chicks always dug me. I started to feel a little guilty when the women would talk to Doug just to get to me. But I do the same for him in a heartbeat. Doug and I have gone to the breeders Mecca in Chicago and I've danced with girls and guys all night long that would never be attracted to me just so Doug could get some play. He's also been to all the gay bars with me and opened himself up to people that without meeting me, he never would have. When it comes to Doug and me, we are very gracious to one another.

Doug grabbed me and gave me a big hug, a little thank you for bringing him to meet his new lover. He asked me what my plan was for the evening and I told him that I was going to The Ten, whether they wanted to come with or not. Doug, my protector, insisted that they accompany me and Markell was totally up for a little women watching. She even volunteered to help me pick up chicks which gave me a laugh, but maybe was the support I needed to help meet someone. As we got ready, my excitement grew at the possibilities of the night. It's always a rush meeting someone new, having that *I'm into you* vibe. A good feeling of being wanted and wanting back. Doug and I made our signature drinks, toasted to new women and out the door we went.

We jumped in my car, and I patiently took directions from Markell as to the location of the lesbians. She actually had been there once before but didn't remember too much from an excess of alcohol. Of course—the one bar marked with the gay flag, there's no way I could miss it. The actual door to the club was through the back parking lot, and as we entered it, my stomach did a little flip. I was excited and nervous. When it comes to women, gay women, I'm way too shy. I've never picked up a girl in my life, except once for a bet during the Chicago Gay Games week. I just, still, after years of being wanted by lesbians everywhere, do not naturally think that women will like me in a sexual way, and am oblivious as to when they are hitting on me. Luckily, women have the guts to talk to me, or in the case of having my great support team— they would initiate conversation.

Wow, this bar reminded me of a strip club! Get me a beer! There was a dance floor, a long bar, and maybe twenty small tables surrounding the dance floor with a good crowd of women sitting at them. We grabbed a table, settled in, and took in the surroundings. All ages, all types, but not like the women in Chicago that I would be more familiar seeing. There was a little something Indiana to these lesbians. Which, in coming from Chicago, meant a little different. Markell dragged me onto the dance floor—don't get me wrong, I love to dance, but up on stage, with all these new women to look at me and nowhere to hide—I was done after one dance. Plus, the way the women were dancing, honestly frightened me a little. These women were, um, interesting. I brought Markell back to the table and left her with Doug while I went to walk around.

I'm very comfortable going to bars alone, I actually enjoy it and often do in Chicago. I like the free feeling of having a couple beers by myself with time to think, talk to the bartender and maybe even socialize with a few regulars. I have my usual bars in Chicago that I fit right in at, where I go to unwind after a night at work or where I know the bartenders and like going up to the bar and they already know my drink. So when I went for a walk, it felt good to have some me time, and check out the scene. I walked to the other side of the bar to see if there was anything I was missing.

A cute girl caught my eye sitting up at the bar. She had a more familiar feel to me than the other women here, a certain look that I liked. She was more boi-ish than what usually grabs my attention but this didn't stop me from gravitating toward her. I casually stood close to where she was sitting while I checked out who else was around me. I could barely finish observing a few women before Doug and Markell were back at my side bringing me another beer. It's okay though, I was having fun with them and for some reason, I didn't want to continue to look for other women, I wanted to talk to the one right next to me. I gently rested my arm on her chair, a bold move for me so I'm sure it was the alcohol in me that put it there. A few femme girls came and danced by us and Doug and Markell both gave me the *go dance with them* look, but something kept me glued to her chair, something magnetic. Doug caught onto my eyes and I gave him the head nod that this girl was the one that had my interest.

Did she initiate a conversation with him or did he with her? I don't know but what I do know is a few seconds later I was talking with her. As I reached out my hand and introduced myself, she giggled at my name and I knew that must be her name, too. Funny, she goes by Jessie and I go by Jess. The conversation flowed easy, or was it just that I had quite the buzz going, and something about her drew me in. She was from Seattle just visiting Indy on a business trip, which explained maybe why there was something different about her than the others, something that brought me over to her chair. I liked her demeanor, her confidence, her friendly eyes. She suggested that we check out another gay bar and I was more than willing to leave The Ten – I had found the best of the bunch, funny that she's from Seattle and not Indy at all.

We all jumped in my car and Markell started us in the direction of the gay bar called Talbott Street. Since having the same name, Doug and I dubbed Jessie as Seattle to not become too confusing. I could tell that he liked her, too, which always raises my interest when getting my best friend's approval. Seattle seemed to know how to get there better than Markell who was just sending us in circles. I was more than willing to trust her. I had no idea where we were! Suddenly, we pulled up to the club. Hot. Seattle was a quick learner, a total turn-on. Every second that passed she became more attractive to me. Attraction for me is so much more than looks, its confidence, eye contact, movement, personality, intelligence. So far, she continually surprised me in a very good way. I already thought she was cute, but getting to know her made her that much more.

Even though I shouldn't have, I had a drink when we got into Talbott Street, that she so kindly bought for me telling me to put my money away. A demanding woman who likes to treat, different for me but oh, so fun. I'm usually the drink buyer, the club finder, the dominator. It took me a little to let go and let her, but it felt comfortable. Doug and Markell went off to make-out and be scandalous and having some alone time with Seattle was just what I wanted. I wanted to kiss her so bad, to see how her lips felt and how she would touch me. I wanted her hands on me, to feel her strength. It happened. And only made me want more and more. Her kisses were addicting and her hands strong. They made me want her to grab my sides and bring me into her. As my mind started fantasizing and my body ached for her, we were interrupted by Doug and Markell. They were ready to go home and make sweet love. I wasn't ready to leave my Seattle surprise so I told her I would meet her back at the bar after I dropped off the dream team. I gave her my telephone number just in case because I knew I didn't want that to be the end of us.

Doug and Markell wanted food before going home but all I could think about was getting back to what Seattle and I had started. Seattle had texted me that I was a hot boi and that she hoped I would come back. Little did she know there's no way I wouldn't be back. I took them straight home and the second they stepped out of the car, I was off in a flash. By this time Seattle had texted me that she was leaving the club and I should meet her at her hotel downtown. I headed in the direction of the tall buildings and my thoughts started racing. Even in my drunken state it didn't keep my mind from reeling from sexual clarity. It was exhilarating. I couldn't stop thinking about her lips back on mine, her hands on me, and my hands on her, in her. I wanted her, to be wanted by her. The heat in my pants was setting fire. How would it be? Two bois, the exchange of control, the fight for the top. I was wet with anticipation.

Don't ask me how I found my way close to her hotel, but I did and then called her to get the exact address. She, being in Indy only for a few days longer than I, directed me right to her doorstep, again, surprising me and her as well on what a good mind she has. There she was, waiting for me at the valet, telling them to park my car and charge it to her room. What a stud. All I could think about on our walk to her room was how much I wanted to explore a more intimate connection with her. The walk seemed to take forever.

Once inside, I had the room to myself to get my bearings and get comfortable while she used the bathroom. Then I took my turn, and when I came out, it was on. I finally got to taste those lips again, and again. She threw me down and tried to take control but I fought back and the wrestling match began. Our kissing and playing proceeded into tossing, hair pulling, biting. Her hands all over my body turned me on. The fight over who would be on top was in full effect. The struggle and affection made me weak for her. At one point I gave into her, laid on my back, let her kiss and bite my body. Her confidence in taking control was hot, her sexual strength and experience evident. She wanted to do whatever I liked, usually what would be my territory. I wanted to please her. I had been craving a woman to take control for the longest time, maybe she was what I quietly dreamed of. Her lips felt so natural on me. I wanted them all over me. I flipped her onto her back, being the sexual gladiator that I was. It made me wet to explore her body with my hands and mouth, to tear off her shirt and get a taste of what's underneath. I was completely comfortable with seeing how far we could take this. I wanted to take her, all of her.

One day it will happen, I know it will. It must. That night, however, she lay on her back and I nestled into her side, fitting perfectly, legs intertwined. She asked me if I was comfortable, what I usually would ask. But surprisingly it felt right to just say yes and cuddle up to her chest. I had a big smile on my face as we passed out quickly.

I woke up alone in the bed and looked over to find her packing up her things. I knew she had an early flight and that our goodbye would be soon, but how do I say it? I wanted more of her, to throw her back down on the bed, kiss her again and dance like we did just a few hours earlier. But maybe that was too much? I quietly got dressed and offered her a ride to the airport, but she already had a car coming for her. I told her I was going to get going then and gave her a few kisses goodbye. I didn't want her forgetting about me just yet.

It took me a good while to get in my car and leave. The hotel staff offered to print me up directions to Markell's house since I had no idea how to get home. I texted her that the hotel staff was being so nice and she asked if I was still there because she was on her way down, but by that time I had already left.

The rest of my weekend in Indy was great fun and consumed by thoughts of her. My Friday night with Seattle was the highlight of my trip. Here I am, a few weeks later still thinking about her, her smile, her lips, her voice. The communication that we've had since then has only made me dig her more. I look forward to her emails more than my favorite television show, and her texts happily fill my inbox. My intrigue about her has grown and my want is escalating.

I know it will happen, one day, Seattle, one day. After all, the seven reminders that you left me all over my body have all but barely faded. It's time for some more boi bruises.

Being Me
By Quay

I'm washing my hands at the sink at the Vitamin Cottage bathroom, when this women walks in. I can see her reflection in the mirror in front of me. She looks at me and says, "I must be in the wrong bathroom!"

Nothing new to me, I have heard that many times. "No you're not—you are in the right bathroom."

She is dressed in a black spaghetti strap top and a black skirt. Probably in her late sixties, mid-seventies. I have on cut off jean shorts and a button down cotton shirt with the sleeves cut off, socks and shoes. The cotton shirt with the sleeves cut off is much cooler to wear than T-shirts in the Santa Fe summer. Plus, I like the way it looks. It works for me.

The woman says I look like a guy. I tell her no I'm a womyn. This is where it gets funny, a new rendition of what usually happens. She says, "You have guy shoes on." I'm amazed she is still going on about the way I'm dressed. I look down at my shoes and say they are hiking shoes and are pretty androgynous. I have never met anyone like her before, who is wanting to be so persistent in trying to make me into a guy. Usually when I hear *oh I must be in the wrong bathroom*, my reply is *no, you're not*, and that is the end of the conversation. But this lady won't give up. I want to say to her, *look lady, don't you think I know what I am?* But instead I tell her I'm butch. Well that ends right there. I leave the bathroom and fill up my water bottles and get in line to pay when I see the lady from the bathroom is in front of me. No eye contact and no more talking. I pay for the water and go out to my truck. Get in and head across the street to Home Depot.

Ok, where is the list of materials I need for today? I'm driving back to Arf women's land with materials to work on Estrella's addition to her cabin. I'm playing over the whole bathroom scene with that woman. I feel really proud of the way I responded. It was just like—oh, I know how to do this without getting angry. I was more amazed that she kept going on about my clothes. Maybe she never met a butch womyn before. I have no idea of her story. So what does being butch mean to me? What is it to be butch? It's me. It's who I am.

Growing up I played outside as much as possible. Me, my older brother and the neighborhood kids. We would play kick ball, whiffle ball, hide and go seek, ride bikes around the neighborhood and set up jumps for our bikes, knock and run, fun kid stuff. My pony, Cocoa, was my adventure buddy. If I was not riding horses with the other kids, Cocoa and I would be off on our own adventure. Sort of like the books I liked reading in fourth or fifth grade, Billy and Blaze. They were always going off on adventures. There was an old dairy farm with a windmill that was abandoned. And lots of acres of fields and woods to ride around in. Running down the old dirt road that went along the railroad tracks at full speed, feeling the wind in my face, that was freedom. I loved that taste of freedom of no one knowing where I was. I just had to be home by dark.

When I was a kid I used to help my dad do projects around the house. I liked being his helper. I remember wanting a cabinet shelf for my 8-track stereo and my albums. One day after school we went down to his work room and laid out the plywood. I got to help him measure and cut the wood and nail it together. We stained it and presto! I had a place for my stereo, albums, and 8-tracks.

I have always worked with my hands. I used to work on sport fishing boats out of Pirate's Cove Marina down in Port Salerno. I was the only female first mate working in that area. I never felt out of place working on boats. I could rig up a ballyhoo or mullet rig just as good as anyone else. And I didn't even know I was butch then!

Carpentry has been my source of income for the past twenty-eight years. I feel competent in what I do. I know how to use a circular saw, a Sawzall, chop saw, table saw. And running up and down ladders is fine for me too. I travel around with a truck full of tools.

Several summers ago, I was doing a remodel job on a cabin at Arf. Wren and I worked together a lot. This was strictly business, as we both had other lovers. We got to be good friends, and on many mornings, she would show up to help. The summer was ending and her cabin was really coming together and I was trying to wrap things up. She would come to me with her charming smile and ask me to do one more thing. And yes, I would.

My butchness is part of me. I'm comfortable in it. Well the dress style for sure is a part of it for me. I have my certain style that I'm comfortable in. I wear men's jeans. I like them much better. They have deeper pockets and wider legs for my work boots. I like the men's button-down shirts too, and I can't forget the cargo shorts and T-shirts. Though I don't want to pass as a guy, I want to pass as me.

Getting dressed up at festival. The dance starts in a half hour. I brought my clothes in from my truck so I can shower and dress in the rowdy cabin. Wendy and Barb and Angela are still getting ready, too. I have my black jeans and I figure out what shirt to wear. It's the white one with color trim that Bonnie brought me back from her Mexico trip last spring. They look good together. My big decision is do I tuck it in or leave it out? So I ask Wendy. She suggests the tucked in look. She says she likes to help a butch get dressed. And yes, I like getting dressed with femmes to go out. Femmes' sweet smiles make this butch melt. And if they smile at me and ask me to help them, I'm right there. Yes I'm attracted to femmes. They catch my eye. I enjoy cooking meals together, I love when they smile at me or wink at me from across the table. I love having coffee in bed and talking. I like that feeling of what happens when we touch. I like that affection from them, and I love that exchange of energy we share. That is what being butch is to me.

On the Politics of Erasure
By Giovanna Capone

Since gaping sores and flaps of skin
are not conducive to walking around
in polite society unnoticed
I'm learning how to sew
They were right when they told us sooner or later
every woman has to

This patchwork scar tissue I'm making
may not be the latest fashion
but it'll have to do, for two reasons

There are worse choices in life
than being unfashionable
besides, this makeshift quilt
is really my original design
recycled for efficiency.

I pledge allegiance to myself
and to the united states of my being.
Look at me now.
At the end of my arm is a blade
I can use it to whittle or slash.
Take your pick.
Either way, I'll be carving my space.

If not carving means I live stooped
into space big enough
for a woman half my size
I'll plan to be carving my entire life.

If not fighting means
I'm towed from my cosmic parking space
at owner's expense
you can all go to hell

tunnel visions physicists
whatever clever form
you take on.

I plan to maintain the solid state
for at least another sixty, seventy years
Fuck you. The only thing doomed to extinction
is your attitude.
I plan to be a soldier my entire life.
Maybe the next soap box I stand on will be your face.
In any case, I hope I never get good
at politely accommodating schrapnel.

So
if not hollering
means I go unheard
then I guess I'll have to shatter
your eardrums.

Not that words
will be my only ammunition.

Definitions
By Giovanna Capone

I wake up alone
to a feeling of edge carving edge
molars grinding against each other, jaws aching
bone tired and sore
these mornings without you
a good sign – torn muscle is rebuilding itself

Rising to my current routine
of fasting, sharpening, refining
I threw out some old clothes
and cut my hair
body pared down
to only the necessities—warm ups, sweatband, barefoot
I begin stretching my legs
extend one, contract the other

What was it you once said?
inching my torso closer and closer
to the floor
the split seconds of feet
sliding over polished wood
the tendons in my thighs straining
I do remember
holding, counting, reverse legs and repeat

You're gone, but
sixteen, seventeen, eighteen
What you said isn't

Now the barbell
twenty curls in standing position
before bench pressing three sets of thirty
flat on my back, gripping the silver bar
hands spread two fists wider than shoulders' length apart

I'm pushing thirty pounds straight up
thirty pounds, thirty times
lift, rest, repeat, rest, repeat

What it was you said
holding for thirty-two, three, four if I'm into it
pushing, pulling

You once told me
edge to edge, packing my muscle against steel, exhausted
You once said

Anything a woman does is feminine
veins bulging, chest heaving, panting, panting

Butch Is a Medium
By Leander Borem

My high school best friends were a butch and a femme. Were. They're not dating anymore, we're not friends anymore, nor are they butch or femme anymore. We thought we were all lesbians. Turns out two of us are bisexual, and I'm the butch after all. It's only been a few years since then— a whirlwind of emotions, desires, identities. A butch and a femme and a best friend. Third wheeling to lesbians, as a lesbian, is a fascinating experience. There is, *was,* so much new queer passion and love and discovery happening next to me, within reach yet certainly not my reach. Still beautiful though, of course. Whether as witness or participant or both, there is a magical lived timelessness with a butch and a femme, following in the footsteps of people with whom history has only allowed me a tenuous connection. I wouldn't be alive in the way that I am today if it weren't for my then-butch and then-femme best friends. I saw the complexities of other queer people experiencing queerness. Their own, each other's for the first time. All too intense, as it always is. No one is ready for the utterly all-consuming realness of being a teenager, especially not queer people who are learning the meaning of embodiment, emotion, and entanglement with others. My then-lesbian, then-best friends were the first world within worlds of queer possibility. Not long after we graduated high school, they broke up. We went three separate ways, geographically, and regarding our queerness, too. Outside of the context of their relationship they ultimately wandered away from the terms butch and femme, while I carefully delved into what I knew of masculine queerness, much of what came from the no-longer-butch. I still carry a lot of them with me in my masculinity. At the time, I believed I was only attracted to women, and my formerly butch friend made the lesbian butch comfortable and familiar already, if only vicariously. Therefore, I adopted the term butch for myself, a tentative foray into a lifetime of queer discovery, and it accompanies me to this day, despite in a different way. Being butch is a medium through which to explore masculine queer embodiments. It allowed me to eventually arrive at my trans identity, and continues to shape how I experience queerness, together and with others. My queerness is always unstable and tending toward new paths, yet I carry butch with me wherever I go, at least so far. Tentative, tender exploration is at the heart of what it means to be queer as a whole, and in my life, butch.

My story of the very beginning
By James

I identify as a Stone Butch and have lived as such for the greatest part of my life. When I look back to my very beginnings, there were many signs of a female bodied masculinity, but perhaps it is in these snippets of my childhood that I now share with you, where I can begin to see where my awareness of gender first began to emerge.

I can clearly recall the emotions of despair that I felt at four years of age when my mother told me that my jeans were to be handed over to my brother as I had now reached the age where I should only be wearing dresses. My protests and outburst resulted in being sent to sit outside on the stairs of our apartment building where I was to stay until I learned how to behave. After sitting, which at the time had felt like hours, I looked up in response to someone asking me about my tears. Standing in front of me was a woman dressed as I should have been, slicked back short hair, open necked collared shirt, and mismatched suit jacket and pants. I explained that I didn't want to wear this, pulling aggressively at the ruffled dress so that it was made clear what offending article had me so distraught. The stranger took her time to smile, but when she did, I felt that I had met my first friend.

"I can understand that, I really can," she said. "However, best that you head back home."

It was such a simple encounter, but the impact was monumental. Suddenly the world had become a little larger. In the months that followed when I would hear my mother mention the "bull dykes" that lived upstairs, though she spoke of them with such seething contempt, disgust permeating with every word, all I would dream of was one day moving to the apartment where girls didn't wear dresses.

Divorce led to a new home and my mother became too occupied to concern herself with what her daughter might be doing or wearing, and I was left to play in the streets. We were now living on the ground floor of a grand house that had been converted into separate dwellings, a business operated upstairs where beautiful women entertained their men friends. On this particular day my mother told me that a lady from the government was coming to see us and schooled me in answers that should be given if asked. She then polished me up, my hair was brushed, and I was put back into a dress. The woman from the government sat at our table drinking tea, and when I was called in, the woman put down her cup and said *come let me look at you, oh, what a beautiful little girl you are!* The impact of these words triggered a projectile vomit, a thick rainbow of colors with odorous chunks covered everything around me including my dress. So, I did next what made the most sense to me, I removed my dress, enthusiastically kicking it across the room, and I now seemed to stand much taller and felt free to smile wearing nothing but white underwear and short socks and black shiny buckle up shoes. I was quickly ushered from the room, and happily went back to playing in the street.

Amongst the kids who I would play with was my best friend, Charlie. One day Charlie excitedly displayed a silver coin earned from the man at the corner grocery store who was offering to pay for help to unload the fruit and vegetable delivery trucks. I of course immediately offered my services but was told that I wasn't strong enough and in response to my demonstration of flexed biceps, the grocery man told me not to be foolish, that *this was not work for a girl.* I knew that I was taller and stronger than Charlie, so I assumed that it was my long hair that was the issue, so I returned with it pulled up and hidden under a hat, which henceforth became my signature accessory throughout my childhood, but was again rejected.

I remember distinctly that feeling of confusion and anger at being told that I was just a girl. On the day, Sheila, one of the women who worked upstairs, after hearing my story kissed me on my cheek and offered to get me a biscuit and glass of milk and brought me to the upstairs living room. I loved visiting that room, it was always full of the most beautiful women who would talk excitedly among themselves, often forgetting that I was there. I would sit quietly in a room that smelled like an exotic garden, watching what seemed to me the artistry of a magician at work as they would spray and coif their hair and apply makeup, while all the time laughing at stories that I didn't understand. To me, each of these women were more beautiful than any storybook princess, and Sheila the most beautiful of all. On this day that stays clearly in my memory, I had been sitting on the sofa next to Sheila watching her apply the red to her lips, when she suddenly and unexpectantly redirected her conversation that she had been having to me and said, "but you little one will never be like that, I know that you will be different and will always treat a lady right". With no idea what she was talking about I nodded in agreement, as I would have done to anything she would have asked of me.

In the grand house, at the very top floor, in an apartment where the ceilings followed the line of the roof, lived my grandmother, and I couldn't have loved anyone more than I did her. My grandmother was fluent in French and English and would often switch back and forth between the two languages in a single conversation. She had lived an extraordinary life worthy of a best-selling novel. My grandmother loved me, a love that came with clear expectations of the behaviors that I was to demonstrate. I was to always stand when a woman did, always offer a woman my seat, and when I got bigger, I was to learn to help her with her coat, and, said my grandmother, if the woman had no coat, I was to offer her mine if there was a chill in the air. I was to always open and hold the door allowing the woman to pass through it first. I was to pick up what she dropped, and at six years old, I knew I was to offer to light a woman's cigarette. My grandmother informed me that I was never to allow a woman to walk on the side of the pavement closest to the road. She took me for a walk to demonstrate why, as we witnessed the passing cars kick up water at the curb-sided pedestrians. My grandmother taught me which fork to use with which course, the appropriate ways to eat different foods, where my elbows went, and that there was no sin in being poor, just acting as though you were. True wealth wasn't measured by coins. Manners, knowing how to behave, she said would open doors and give me access to places and experiences that no amount of money could ever do. And in my grandmother's eyes, as long as I never let my manners fail, I could do no wrong. I could play outside from sunrise till sunset, wear clothes bought for my brother, and donated by friends. I could pretend to be a cowboy, an astronaut, a soldier, a builder, a race car driver. She never reacted when on some evenings, I would sit with her on her bed in her tiny room, and tell her how Tracey wanted to marry me, but was upset that I kissed Sonia. My grandmother said nothing as I explained that I would prefer not to have a wife, just lots of girlfriends. And sometimes she would let me put a little dab of the aftershave she would on occasion wear because she preferred the smell of it, rather than perfume on her skin.

Though I was subject to and lived under the constant threat of the dangers that come from living with alcoholism in the home, and memories of feeling hungry and cold, of the electricity being cut, of no hot water or heat, and early bed-times to keep warm and to try to forget about a grumbling stomach. These times of playing in the streets, dressed in clothes meant for little boys, with stories from my grand-mother, and with real live princesses to talk to, provide some of my happiest memories.

But perhaps from the outside looking in, my life wasn't as it should have been, and a custody battle ensued, and I was taken from the streets and put in the backseat of my father's car. We drove to what I thought was to be a visit to his sister, my aunt, but quickly discovered that I was to say goodbye now also to my father as I was left in what was to become my new home with my aunt, uncle and their four sons. I tried to make sense of my new surroundings, but nothing was familiar, while there was no longer violence to fear, and the house was warm, and meals were guaranteed, I had never felt so alone. The boys, my cousins, my uncle, and I did not enjoy each other's com-pany, for them I was an irritant and interloper, for me they were barbaric, with every behaviour a complete violation of what my grandmother had taught me. My aunt, a beautiful woman who had once been on the front cover of international magazines had long ago become dependant on the bottles that were kept in the well stocked bar. My aunt explained to me that because she knew nothing about raising little girls that it would be better that I be a boy, and with my hair cut and a boy's wardrobe. I was enrolled in school and given a boy's name. Despite not coming with any paperwork, the male principal of my new school accepted me as he found it hard to refuse the pleading request of my aunt, a woman who knew the power that could easily be wielded over a man with ludicrous fanta-sies that she might be available to him.

I discovered later that, rather than having been given

up, I had in fact been taken, and that my identity was changed to avoid been found by my searching grandmother, mother, and the women who worked in the grand house. In time, the courts intervened, and I was returned, but one of the many things I learned from this experience was that I didn't want to be a boy. I was a girl who wanted to act, dress, and behave like me, and me was like how some boys acted, dressed, and behaved. This wasn't a wish or a simple desire, it was who I was, and regardless of how far I was pushed to become the girl that was expected, or the boy that was offered, I would always pull back. Gender norms demanded that I make the choice of being either a feminine girl or a masculine boy, but it takes a child to know when neither fit. This understanding sat comfortably with me, and other children seemed to take it in their stride, boys happy to wrestle with me in the dirt, and the occasional girl sending me a letter declaring their forever love. It was however the parents, the teachers and of course my own mother who made it clear that I was a problem, that there was something not right about me. As I aged and entered teen years my resolve was seriously challenged, as the accepting children of the past disappeared, and were replaced by teens who now echoed the beliefs of their disapproving parents. But that's a story for another day.

Forgiving Seeds
by Calliope Rose

When we first met, she didn't know herself as butch. She was a baby bird, all anxiety and pained tugging at her shirt sleeves, emerging from her room in secondhand Levi's. She was nervous and flighty and had never read Leslie Feinberg or Joan Nestle or any of the rest. She looked at herself in the mirror and saw herself as the daughter disappointment, a failed woman. When we met, I was desperate to be in love. I saw her in a starched white button-down, laughing. I saw her broad shoulders, her crisp buzzcut, and saw myself prepared to strike. I had sprung from the earth fully formed, it seemed. The femme come to shatter her tenuous illusions of self, of the world, of love.

When we first met, she thought the bulk of her rebellion lay in polos and referring to herself as *inactive* when her stepmother begged her to come to church. Mormon guilt stuck with her long after faith had died out. And anyway, how could she show her face on hallowed ground, when I was at her side, all painted lips and excessive cleavage? She flushed and fell apart when I wore a skirt in the wind and let the breeze reveal pink lace, worn especially for her. She would not touch me, despite the wanting. But I sat on her couch all the same, daisy-dukes in the summer heat so that the pleather seat stuck to my thighs and her father looked on, disapproving.

I barreled on, full steam ahead toward devotion. I saw it in her, the tiniest seedling of butch bravado, and I was a determined, foolish gardener. When she finally caved to her own desires, she did so with a sob in the back of her throat and I held her for what felt like an eternity, painted nails raking along her scalp. I thought, this is our foundation, the soil from which we may grow. And for a time, the sun shone down on that little patch of dirt and we flourished. I lifted for her new button-downs and discount joggers and took her to the park for picnic dates. She kissed me in public, cheeks burning crimson as she struggled not to care. I kissed her back, until my lipstick was planted on her cheek like a tattoo. I cinched in at the waist and wore heels despite the muddiness of monsoon season. She always looked at me with a question at the tip of her tongue, though she wouldn't say it out loud.

Why are you like this?

And I didn't have the seven dollars it cost to buy Stone Butch Blues, but I did have my mother's printer and a whole heap of free time. I spent an afternoon punching holes and stringing twine through paper while my toenails dried and kissed along the margins. I held its weight in my hand and whispered to it as though I were summoning its spirit forth, hoping for guidance. Hoping for revelation. I handed it off to her, a massive stack of black and white, on our next date. I wrote a note in pink gel pen on the inside title page:

So you might someday understand.

It's been nearly five years to the day and now I think that seedling has finally started to sprout, wide-eyed and uncertain, from the dark soil. She finally tossed her old prom dress, after carting it around for a decade like some ghost plucked from another millennia. When we first met, she didn't know herself, and now she has chosen a new name, with a new life to go with it. She found her way, stumbling through the dark, once her father fell ill and her stepmother stopped extending Sunday invitations. Nowadays, she chooses my nail color for me, and calls me a good girl when I've got them freshly painted.

I wonder, sometimes, how she looks back on those early days of courtship. I wonder if she gives her seedling self any grace at all, or else looks down on her in shame. I wonder if she looks back and frets over lost time or imagines that we were doomed from the start. I wonder if she feels like a perpetual project. Despite all my wondering, she still lays beside me at night with her tattooed arm draped over my waist. Despite it all, she still sits dutifully on the side of our tub every two weeks while I run her buzzer over the sides of her head. And I think, now, she finally understands.

I see it best when we're fucking, naturally. According to her old pals, it's all I ever saw in her, as though my desires rendered me near biblical. A vixen or harlot come to ruin her. But it's true! Because though she used to shrink in embarrassment at the thought of being desired, it has always been what drove me to her. Sometimes, I wonder if that's what makes me femme, at the heart of it all. My desire for butches, like a lighthouse, has always guided me. But when we first met, and we first made love, she ran her hands over my body and then ran to the bathroom, to scrub herself clean. Not of me, but of her own desires—those unnamable villains, not to be acted on.

After that, I thought, maybe this was some failed experiment. Or maybe I had guessed wrong, and this wasn't the love I had been seeking. Maybe this seedling is little more than a weed, a chore I have tasked myself with despite it never bearing fruit.

But time has a way of healing wounds as much as it forms new ones. And as the years fell away, and I grew my garden up from the verdant earth, she found that desire could lead her home, too. She found herself, for the first time, allowing herself to be desired. And through that, a freedom to feel her own desire, which bloomed from her chest, abundant.

So now when she fucks me, it's as though she has become a full-fledged redwood. The boundless trunk of her expands in all directions, her branches thick and laden with soft leaves, forever reaching for the sun. I call her Leo, which, it should come as no surprise, is not her given, Christian name, or Sir, or Daddy, or whatever other gender-fucked delight she may concoct. She ties me down. She beats me, often at my request. And when we fuck, her strap may as well be an extension of her own body, her own self, shooting into me with abandon.

Nowadays, butchness rolls off of her in waves, and she knows it as her birthright. She grows up from the soil like her toes are buried so deep, her roots so extensive and bound up in the earth that she could never be ripped asunder. Her eyes hold no clouds, the same brilliant blue as the springtime sky, all cheer, all strength. Once a week, I wipe her arm down with rubbing alcohol and press a cool needle into her flesh. Testosterone slips along, a gentle stream toward the roaring waves. And she glows the same way an oak leaf seems to radiate with the sunlight it's absorbed. Chlorophyll bubbles shifting under skin.

Nowadays, when I call myself femme, it is irrevocably relational. My Butch—and she always looks on with a smile when I write it with that big B, as though it's a part of her name— has taught herself rituals of love and liturgy and has taken herself to a new sort of church. She wears Old Spice and plans for top surgery, a mountain of newness she has climbed with vigor. So, now I wish to look back on the trajectory of her life like a topographical map. I want to plot this baptismal emergence from the world before, the growth of the old forest stretching into the future, open-limbed and hungry for life. I want to show her the winding rivers, the hills and valleys which make her. I want her to see how her own roots have grown, how her body has become a harbinger to new life.

She will not be touched, still, though that rolling stone has landed at my feet and found home all the same. No tree can survive, I think to myself, without the rough edges of bark which protect it. Still, hose desires bubble forth, and she shivers and shakes like she's caught in a windstorm. She can't help the uncertainty.

She is still forgetting shame.
She is still forgiving seeds.

The Man My Father Made Me
By Orlando Silver

I am the man my father made me. Which is to say, I am a good man.

He does not know this about me. He looks at me sideways sometimes, quietly considering the way my facial hair is growing in. Nothing is said about it, as is our family tradition.

I am here for dinner, but he shows me the garden first, the new plantings. The way the agapanthus are already in bloom. The new callistemon. The warm, spreading jacaranda boughs.

The two magnolias he planted to remember my dead mother by are budding, slowly. The white blooms will come soon like handfuls of snow, shining bright against the summer air.

My mother always was a paradox that way.

He asks me about the car, my friends, my job.

"Important work, that," he says, thinking of the ways I hold the hands of people in the dark, as they work with thoughts of suicide and crisis. He is thinking also of himself and the precipice of loneliness. I am thinking of myself the same way.

We have both walked those dark paths and told almost nobody about those landscapes.

He asks me about my partner and I say, "Oh. I'm not sure about it. At the moment we are friends."

There is a pause as I silently flail in heartache, and he witnesses. We look at each other with sorrow, knowing there are oceans of words to say.

"Well. You have to take a chance, don't you. On these things," he says, instead.

We talk about family. The worries of older relatives, the way we both drive to the houses of people we love to make sure they are okay. We are concerned about my brother who can't find work. We worry over his sister and her anxiety.

Quietly, over dinner, we both feel the third presence of

his cancer at the table. It is swimming through his bloodstream in a trail of fishhooks. He knows, and I know, that after February when the radiation starts, I will be at his house often, cooking and driving him, and sitting with him for company.

Instead, he tells me about the older woman from church who brings him money every month to buy biscuits for the fellowship morning tea. My father hosts this morning tea of course. The Minister rarely comes but it is more popular than the service. Tea and coffee and cakes are laid out just so. There are tables with decorations. For Christmas, he had a tree. People come and stay. They stay for hours.

My father holds the space. Sets up and packs down. After his first cancer operation, he came back to find the women waiting. All the older women fussed over him and told him to sit, not to carry anything, not to move. He didn't like it.

"I don't know what I'm doing when I don't have people to care for," he says, and I wonder when he got so old, and how we are so much the same.

He says then that the older woman who pays for biscuits has died, suddenly, and he begins to cry. We both do, a little.

"She had a good innings. Meryl was her name. Her son came to tell me. I told him about the biscuits, but he knew, he already knew. He knew all about me, too. If you can make it to ninety-seven you're doing okay. That's what I reckon."

"You're doing a good thing, Dad," I say. "Making a space like that for people." He reaches across the table and he takes my hand.

"Sometimes," he says. "I find it very hard to trust God."

I think, *well, I don't trust him, not really, but I do trust you, Dad.*

The words are in my throat to say but I can't say them. I want to say, *Dad, I am your son. I am so proud to be your son. I don't know how to tell you that I booked the surgery this week to change my body forever, and that I don't want breasts anymore because I want to look like me.*

I don't know how to explain that the hormones I'm taking will change the face he remembers and rob him of the daughter he loved.

I don't know how to ask if he will still love me, and

how long I have left to ask. How long can I hedge my bets and hold my truth to my heart instead.

"Think it'll rain?" he says, looking out at graying skies.

"Depends on the weather," I joke, an old favourite of his.

He laughs, a brilliant open sound that bursts my heart with joy.

"That's a good one," he says, and smiles, letting go of my hand.

Acknowledgments

To the stone butches and the studs,
the diesel dykes, bulldykes, land dykes, and baby dykes,
to the sporty butches, soft butches, and old school butches,
and to everyone else who has ever been brave enough to call
themselves a butch.

And to my wife, Chris, who handles this butch with gentle hands
and still swoons when I wear a baseball cap.

Author Biographies

Ash

Ash is a Political Science MA student researching conspiracy theories and disinformation. They've been doing art as a hobby for more than 10 years in a variety of mediums. They are still exploring what butchness means to them, and finding ways to celebrate butchness in themself and others.

This piece represents discovering my butch identity, and the complicated, overwhelming feelings that came with that. I found love for my body that I never had before I realized I was butch.

Embracing butchness helped unravel the contradiction I experienced in finding people with my body type attractive, but not finding myself attractive.

Merril Mushroom

I am an old-timey bar dyke and present-day land dyke. My publications include many stories about the lesbian bar culture during the 1950's and 1960's, some speculative fiction, and a variety of other articles and stories.

Faith Mosley

Faith Mosley was born and raised in the Midwest. Over the years, she has been blessed with a bunch of wildly diverse jobs to feed her writing habit - from dishwasher to AmeriCorps recruiter. Her work has been included in the short story anthology *Lez Talk: A Collection of Black Lesbian Short Fiction* (BLF Press, 2016), and her first novel, *Sky Court* (Circuit Breaker Books, 2022), was released last November.

Gwendolyn Bikis

I am the author of *Your Loving Arms*, a novel published by Haworth Press; and of *Cleo's Gone,* a novella anthologized in *Does Your Mama Know?, The Persistent Desire, Hers3,* and several editions of *The Best Lesbian Erotica.* I am completing a book of short stories about Oakland CA, entitled *Dog's Dogs.*

The success of this essay owes largely to my writing group: Jennifer, Terry, Brigitte, and Faith.

Mary E. Cronin

Mary E. Cronin writes fiction and poetry from her home on Cape Cod in Massachusetts. She spent her early years in the Bronx, NY, where she fell in love with reading, writing, and libraries. Mary's poems have been published in numerous children's anthologies, and her poetry for adults has been published in *Provincetown Magazine, Hashtag Queer* vol. 2, and *The New York Times.*
As a student of history and a lesbian educator and poet, she seeks to bring underrepresented voices and untold stories to the page. Mary is represented by Lori Steel of Red Fox Literary. You can find her at www.maryecronin.com.

Georgie Orion

Georgie Orion (she/her) is a butch/MOC lesbian living in a midwestern college town. Georgie delights in being called he, sir, and, even once, a gentleman, by strangers and claims she completed her PhD just so she could use Dr. instead of a gendered honorific. Georgie loves suit jackets and lapel pins. She loves plaid shirts and plaid shorts but has promised her wife she won't wear them both at the same time. Georgie is a mother, a sister, a professor, a gardener, a horizontal filer, and a retired roller derby skater. She is remarkably skilled at catching frogs.

Abby Cohen

Abby Cohen was the owner and manager of Abby's BookCase, a used bookstore of some note, for twenty-five years. More recently, she has been proud to be on the board of Creative Light Factory, which was a studio for writers. She can be found every Thursday at Steel City Coffeehouse in Phoenixville performing her stories at open mic, as well as various songs by other people. She is currently trying to decide what to do when she grows up. She usually writes memoir, but has been known to dabble in fiction occasionally.

Cerys Meredith

1978, wife and two children, Antwerp area, Belgium. Songwriter, guitarist and singer. Sometimes I just write. Soft butch, I think. But you know, whatever.

Virginia Black

Virginia Black's work includes short stories with Sapphire Books as part of their FANDOM TO FANTASY series, "Constant" in the GCLS Writing Academy anthology WRITING FREEDOM, and "Reclamation" in the Bold Strokes Books anthology "IN OUR WORDS - Queer Stories from Black, Indigenous, and People of Color Writers." Her debut novel, CONSECRATED GROUND, was recently published by Bywater Books, and features a badass war witch of rakish beauty who hunts vampires with spellcraft. Virginia Black lives in the Pacific Northwest with her wife and daughter and is always hoping for rain. Learn more at virginiablackwrites.com.

Cindy Rizzo

Cindy Rizzo is a NYC-based author of five novels, plus short stories and essays. The first two books of her young adult speculative fiction trilogy, *The Papercutter* and *The Border Crosser*, were published by Bella Books in 2021 and 2022. Her novel, *Exception to the Rule*, won the 2014 Goldie for Best Debut Author. Her short stories and essays have appeared in anthologies and on Medium.com. Cindy publishes a newsletter of curated content for authors and readers of Sapphic fiction. She serves on the board of GCLS is a consultant to social justice philanthropy.

Victoria Anne Darling

Victoria Anne Darling is a low maintenance high femme, author of three stone-sexuality-focused books and one children's picture book that features a gender and racially ambiguous kid exploring pronouns and identities with high self-esteem. Victoria kayaks and tent camps, jumps out of airplanes, dresses to dazzle, listens for more than what's said, recognizes consent (verbal *and* nonverbal), and loves emotionally deep conversations that allow everyone to connect meaningfully, beyond the superficial. She is known for the directness of her gaze, the tenderness of her heart, and her butch-loving femininity.

Giovanna Capone

Giovanna Capone is a poet, fiction writer, playwright, editor, & filmmaker from an Italian neighborhood near the Bronx. She now lives in the San Francisco Bay Area. Bedazzled Ink published her first book, *In My Neighborhood: Poetry & Prose.* Her play, "Her Kiss", was performed for sold-out audiences in San Francisco by Luna Sea Women's Performance Project. She has co-edited two anthologies: *Hey Paesan! Writing by Lesbians & Gay Men of Italian Descent,* and *Dispatches from Lesbian America: 42 Short Stories & Memoir by Lesbian Writers.* Giovanna is a public librarian. Her new film is called: *Finding the Italians: A Granddaughter's Journey.* www.giovannacapone.weebly.com

Susan Spilecki

I came out late, in 2015, which gave me access to the word butch, finally allowing me to recognize myself. I teach writing at Northeastern University and MIT. My poetry has been nominated for the Pushcart Prize and published in such journals as *Frontiers, Quarterly West, Quarter After Eight, Potomac Review, Midwest Poetry Review,* and the 2023 anthology *Beyond Queer Words*. More of my work can be seen at www.buildingapoem.com.

Steph Ban

Steph Ban is new to both claiming butch as an identity and writing memoir for publication. Her independent, interdisciplinary scholarship can be found in such places as *The Activist History Review, Disability Studies Quarterly,* and *Voices: A World Forum for Music Therapy*. She would like to thank the following people for their support with this piece: friend Lilith A. Siegel, partner Emmalie Hall-Skank, self-described token ostensibly non-queer cishet dude Andrew Dell Antonio, and Elizabeth (Ibby) Grace (the first butch she ever met).

Zeeb

Zeeb is a psychotherapist, a former summer camp director, and an avid international traveler. She came out as a lesbian in 1971. A daughter of second wave feminism, she fashioned her own identity as androgynous/butch. This worked until menopause, when she started putting on weight in all the feminine places, so now she can only pull off soft-butch. Her lesbian bona fides include owning a respectable amount of power tools, having several pair of Birkenstocks to wear for any occasion, previously owning both a truck and a Subaru, and having submitted to the domination of multiple cats over her lifetime.

Susa Silvermarie

Spoken word artist Susa Silvermarie is a widely published and anthologized writer known for original work that delights the senses while calling the spirit. Silvermarie is grateful to live her third trimester of life on the shore of Lake Chapala in Ajijic Mexico. She shares her work and would love to have you visit her at www.susasilvermarie.com Two of her collections are available on Amazon: *Tales from My Teachers on the Alzheimer's Unit,* and, *Poems for Flourishing,* with a third collection forthcoming later this year.

John Dominic

In 1946, John Dominic emerged from the womb a butch lesbian in her birthday suit. This was the first of many suits she would wear with pride. Early on, she showed a propensity for masculine dress. A 1972 transplant from NY to CA, she reflects east coast sensibilities. She lives her lesbian feminist values as a separatist, who has a few male friends. Before retiring as a teacher, reading specialist and educational administrator, she assiduously integrated women's history and contributions into all aspects of the curricula. She holds degrees from Fordham, Pepperdine and Santa Clara Universities.

Rowan Harvey

Rowan Crow Harvey is a twenty-year-old butch lesbian living in Iowa City while she figures out what she wants to do with her life. She loves writing, sewing, and working outdoors. When she's not engaging in any of her many hobbies, she spends her time drinking coffee on the couch with her femme lesbian girlfriend and their two dogs.

M.A. Dubbs

M. A. Dubbs is an award-winning Mexican American and LGBT+ writer who hails from Indiana. For more than a decade her writing has been published in literary magazines and anthologies across the globe. In 2022 she released her first chapbook, *An American Mujer,* with Bottlecap Press, was nominated for a Pushcart Prize from *Oyster River Pages,* and served as a judge for Indiana's state Poetry Out Loud competition.

Claudia R. Asch

Claudia R. Asch (b. 1977) is now unapologetically butch and queer. They were born and raised in Germany, by American parents. They finally embraced their queerness in 2020, at the height of the COVID-19 pandemic. They completed a Bachelor of Arts at Tufts University in Medford, Massachusetts, USA and Masters and PhD at Syracuse University, Syracuse, NY, USA. They live in Brighton, UK with their wife, four cats, and a dog, and work in the brewing industry.

S.E. Smyth

S.E. Smyth is putting words into the world. The stories she tells are never exactly how they happened. Elusive as she proclaims she is, you can usually find her nose buried in primary sources plotting a story. Despite persisting historical references, she wholeheartedly believes she lives in the present. In addition to writing, she carries heavy things for her wife, rubs cat bellies, and can often be seen taking brisk walks. The household is certain there is something odd going on. She and her wife travel when the air is right looking for antique stores, bike trails, and breathtaking beaches.

Gabby Cohen

Gabby (they/she) is the founder of the Butch Boudoir Project, a photography and autobiographical project elevating butch identity through their own story and experience. Along with the #ButchCrew, Gabby is shaking things up by dismantling the binary and celebrating nontoxic masculinity across a spectrum of gender. Gabby is a Non-Binary Queer Butch who is passionate about creating space for community, inclusivity, and butch visibility. Gabby is a business owner, talented artist, incredible wife, queer parent, and activist.

Beck Guerra Carter

Beck Guerra Carter (they/she) is a butch poet from Austin, Texas. They have their MFA from Texas State University and have been published in *Lavender Review*, the lickety-split, and Odes and Elegies: Eco-Poetry from the Texas Gulf Coast. Their life is more than a list of failures and accomplishments. So is yours.

Missouri Vaun

Missouri Vaun is a two-time Golden Crown Literary Society award-winning lesbian romance writer. Strong connections to her roots in the rural South have been a grounding force throughout her life. Vaun spent twelve years finding her voice working as a journalist in places as disparate as Chicago, Atlanta, and Jackson, all along filing away characters and their stories. Her novels are heartfelt, earthy, and speak of loyalty and our responsibility to others.

Her alter ego is cartoonist Paige Braddock, creator of Eisner-nominated comic strip, Jane 's World, the first gay-themed comic work to receive online distribution by a national media syndicate in the U.S.

She and her wife live in Northern California. Find out more at missourivaun.com and pb9.com.

Jen T. Stoughton

Jen Stoughton (she/her) is a writer and filmmaker originally from Maryland and currently based in Los Angeles. She has been a softball-playing, short-hair-having, flat-out lesbian since before she knew what those words meant and likes to approach her butchness with joy and humor. She explores themes of identity, self-actualization, and queer joy in her work.

Rebecca Ritts

Hello, my name is Rebecca Ritts. I wrote this many years ago about the first woman I fell in love with, who was (obviously) butch. Although that relationship is in my past, the love and admiration I have for butches is not! I am now happily married and I'm the femme to my butch wife. We live in Annapolis MD with our two fur-babies: Oliver and Liesel. I am a mother, a daughter, a wife, a sister, an aunt, and a fiercely Proud Femme.

Kristin Schloemer

Hi! My name is Kristin Schloemer. I live in Cedar Rapids, Iowa, and work as a Licensed Mental Health Counselor. My family includes two beautiful sons and the love of my life, Jody. I enjoy binging TV, cuddling with my cats, and sleeping. My passions include humor, music, and writing, and I'm intrigued by deep conversations and connections made between people. I value the vulnerability of sharing thoughts and feelings and why people do what they do (myself included). I continue to learn what it takes to find and be myself in a world that would rather I not.

Rae Theodore

Rae Theodore (she/they) is the author of the poetry chapbook *How to Sit Like a Lesbian* and the memoirs *My Mother Says Drums Are for Boys: True Stories for Gender Rebels* and *Leaving Normal: Adventures in Gender*. Her work has been nominated for

Best of the Net and the Pushcart Prize. Rae lives in Royersford, Pennsylvania, with her wife, who has mastered the art of butch appreciation.

Xequina Ma. Berber

Xequina was telling stories by first grade, and writing them as soon as she could put a sentence together. She has a Master's in Women's Spirituality, is a librarian, and has also worked as a journalist, columnist, and immigration paralegal. She was an editor for *Dispatches from Lesbian America* (2017) and published a collection of lesbian short stories, *The Only Female Cross-Dresser in Memphis* (2021). Xequina speaks Spanish fluently, is a traditional Mexican healer, paints, and loves to cook. She lives in Oakland with her partner of fourteen years and three ungrateful cats.

JD Voss

JD Voss is a masculine of center, gender fluid, she/he/they, ever evolving tender-hearted cowboy. A successful Restaurateur and Chef, JD loves to use food and drink to build community and create safe spaces that leave people feeling warm-all-over, in a tight hugged kind of way.

JD is an athlete, thrill seeker, dog papa, dad joke teller and bucket list adventurer who is blood and chosen family centered. They thrive in and crave traveling to learn new cultures and see how people live and eat all over the world.

Ultimately, JD is passionate about sharing moments with people on this journey called life, that are the simple somethings that mean everything.

Quay Zee

I came out as a lesbian in my early 20s when I was working on a charter boat on Nantucket, Massachusetts, in the 80s. I spent the majority of my summers from late 20s until into my 40s working the womyn festival circuit mostly on the east coast. Back then there were many and much longer than a weekend. And what a way to connect with other lesbians. I have lived most of my life on womyns land in the Ozarks between Missouri and Arkansas, which is where I fell in love with kayaking and canoeing the many beautiful rivers and creeks. Now I live at Arf outside Santa Fe, New Mexico, where I have built my own cabin, which is totally off the grid (first I had to tear down a rodent-infested cabin). I love the land and the community. I spend the winter down at Lake Annie outside Gainesville, Florida. For the most part, I do handy womyn work for a living and have built many houses on different womyns lands.

Leander

Leander (they/he) is a Brazilian trans artist and writer currently living in NYC. Their recent work primarily explores emergent relationships between queerness, disability, embodiment, and time. Through mediums in writing and visual arts such as poetry and painting, his experiences as an autistic person are given shape as self-evident explorations of being.

James

James has run a dual career in tandem, one in theatre the other in academics. Today, James continues their postdoc work in bioethics with a particular focus on gender norms and identities. Having equally divided their fifty+ years on the planet living in the UK, US, Australia, and Canada, James grew up in a time that saw the Butch-Femme community flourish and then watched it move underground only later to reemerge. James prefers the hy/ hym pronouns and is comfortable with labels such as OFOS, Dom, and Stone, but has always and will always be Butch- the noun. James runs an active blog at www. https:// www.butchdayz.com/

Calliope Rose

Calliope Rose is a white, fat, high femme writer currently living on unceded Mississauga and Potawatomi land. She creates erotic pieces centering the experiences of femme4butch sensuality and romance. Her work focuses on themes of domination and submission, devotion, personal embodiment, and occasionally, lesbian vampires. When not writing, Calliope spends most of her time baking, reading, and pretending to be a bona-fide film scholar to anyone who will listen. Her work can be found on Medium, Patreon, and Instragram @femme4feelings.

Orlando Silver

Orlando Silver (he/they) lives and writes on Dharug land, in Australia. They are a playwright, performer and community activist. He can be found on substack: https://orlandosilver.substack.com/ or on Instagram as @orlando_silver_

Bringing rainbow stories to life.

Flashpoint Publications welcomes submissions from writers of every color and books featuring characters of every color. In addition, Flashpoint Publications encourages job applicants of every color whenever a staff position becomes available. We believe that EVERYONE is entitled to a seat at our table.

www.flashpointpublications.com